Maria Elena is the pro
Spanish grandee at the court of Elizabeth I. She is passionately torn between her love for a Scots privateer – the formidable Adam MacDonald – and loyalty to the men he has sworn to kill – her own father and brother. Against the turbulent background of 1586, with Philip of Spain massing his men and ships for an invasion of England and her own father secretly plotting to assassinate the Queen, Maria Elena is a fragile pawn in the political game. She finds herself facing a charge of high treason – or life with a man who has sworn he will never love her in return.

By the same author in Masquerade

FRANCESCA
MADELON
GAMBLER'S PRIZE
A PRIDE OF MACDONALDS
THE COUNTESS

Maria Elena
Valentina Luellen

MILLS & BOON LIMITED
London · Sydney · Toronto

First published in Great Britain 1968 by
Wright & Brown Ltd., 18 Stukeley Street,
London W.C.2

This edition published 1980 by
Mills & Boon Limited,
London W1

© Valentina Luellen 1968
Australian copyright 1980
Philippine copyright 1980

ISBN 0 263 73223 1

This book is sold subject to the condition that it shall not, by way of trade or otherwise, be lent, re-sold, hired out or otherwise circulated without the prior consent of Mills & Boon Limited in any form of binding or cover other than that in which it is published and without a similar condition including this condition being imposed on the subsequent purchaser.

The text of this publication or any part thereof may not be reproduced or transmitted in any form or by any means, electronic or mechanical, including photocopying, recording, storage in an information retrieval system, or otherwise, without the written permission of the Publishers.

Filmset in 10 on 11½pt Plantin

Made and printed in Great Britain by
C. Nicholls & Company Ltd,
The Philips Park Press, Manchester

The author acknowledges grateful thanks to the Harmsworth Encyclopaedias, from which many of the historical facts in this novel came.

This above all – to thine own self be true,
And it must follow, as the night the day,
Thou canst not then be false to any man.
Hamlet, Act 1, Scene 3

CHAPTER ONE

THE thirteenth of August in the year 1586 was a pleasantly warm autumn day, and for the first time in over a month, Mary Stuart was allowed to leave the house at Chartley, her prison for the last eighteen months, to go hunting. She loved the thrill of the chase and the company of her friends on occasions like this, but since she had fled from Scotland and been placed under the guardianship of her cousin Elizabeth, Queen of England, the happy moments had been all too few.

Eighteen years of constant imprisonment had taken their toll of Mary's looks and physical strength. Her frail body, racked with rheumatism, was growing steadily weaker and several times over the past months she had completely lost the use of her hands and been confined to bed. Two things about her remained steadfast, untouched by ill-health or imprisonment. Her claim to the English throne on the grounds of Elizabeth's illegitimacy and her staunch Catholic faith, which in times of stress was her only consolation.

From a thin, pale face, dark eyes stared at the passing countryside. She wore a sombre grey dress, severe in its simplicity, the stark lines broken only by the gold crucifix around her neck. Her long red hair was neatly plaited and coiled around her head and covered by a long black veil.

She felt neither the warmth of the sun on her cheeks, nor the excitement which had first gripped her at these unexpected moments of freedom. Where was her faithful friend, Anthony Babington? It had been two weeks since he had last smuggled a letter to her in one of the wine casks sent each week for her ladies-in-waiting and secretaries. Daily she expected to hear of Elizabeth's death at the hands of the young Irishman or one of his friends; she prayed for their success in her devotions, yet still there was no news. Was England never to be free from the yoke of her Protestant cousin?

Across the Channel lay the Netherlands under the rule of Philip of Spain, an ally near at hand to help her when the time came and across the border in Scotland, there were more loyal Catholics willing to flock to her banner. If only the shadow of Elizabeth did not hover over all her plans.

They were almost to the gates of Foxall, a wealthy estate where she assumed the hunt would begin. Its border lay alongside Chartley and it was not a great distance from her prison itself. She was never allowed to go far for her jailors feared her friends might attempt a rescue. This was in Mary's mind as she caught sight of someone moving in the trees ahead. Horsemen – at least a dozen. Babington! He had come to tell her Elizabeth was dead. Mary Stuart was Queen of England at last; the dreams were to become reality.

"Madam, you are to come with us."

The unsmiling face which presented itself at the carriage window was not that of Anthony Babington. Mary's heart grew cold with fear at the sight of her cousin's insignia on the jacket of the man before her. The Queen's personal guard. What had brought them so far from her side to interrupt the pleasantness of her outing? Before she could utter a word the answer was made known to her.

"I have a signed order from Her Most Gracious Majesty, Elizabeth of England. You are to be escorted to Tixall, Madam, to await the Queen's pleasure."

Mary knew that Babington would not come now. He had either been arrested or he was dead. The ache in her heart was like the slow twisting of a knife. So real was the pain that she winced. Suddenly it became horribly clear why she was to be detained elsewhere. Her possessions were to be searched, letters read and misinterpreted.

The helplessness of her position brought tears to her eyes, yet somehow she held them back. She, too, was a Queen in her own right, these men would see no sign of weakness from her. For a moment her dark eyes rested on the face of her constant companion Sir Amyas Paulet and silently condemned his betrayal. He was one of her jailors, but she had grown to like him and had begun to think of him more as a friend than an enemy. Then her gaze flickered past him and came to rest coldly, disdainfully on the captain-in-charge.

"I wish you a fruitless search, gentlemen," she said humourlessly, and moved away from the window to the far side of the carriage.

On the twenty-eighth of August, after two long weeks of being under close guard, deprived of her secretaries Nau and Curle, refused the use of pen and ink and paper and allowed only two ladies-in-waiting, Mary was returned to Chartley. She had long since ceased to be outraged at the treatment she had received and even the sight of her disarranged apartments, the ransacked cabinets with their broken locks and the realisation most of her private papers were missing, failed to rouse her to an outburst of temper.

She stood for a long while in the doorway of the ransacked study with Amyas Paulet standing ill at ease a few feet away. He had been her friend once, like Darnley, her own sweet Bothwell, George Douglas who had aided her escape from Lochleven, little twisted Rizzio and countless others whose nameless faces plagued her dreams and induced such terrible nightmares she would waken in the night soaked with sweat. How many more would pass through her life into obscurity without knowing her gratitude for their great sacrifices? Long, painfully thin fingers closed around the crucifix at her throat and a strange, almost peaceful expression settled over Mary's face. With immense dignity she said:

"There are two things not even your precious Elizabeth can take from me. I am a Queen in my own right; royal blood runs in my veins and my faith is that of my fathers — and will remain so until God sees fit to take me from this earth."

A few days later Mary Stuart was removed to Fotheringay Castle in Northamptonshire, unaware of the commission set up in London to acquire proof of her treasonous relationship with Anthony Babington and other conspirators, at that moment imprisoned in the Tower, and thus involve her without shadow of doubt in the plot to murder Elizabeth.

A change of air would do her good, Sir Amyas Paulet told her, and perhaps lessen the rheumatism which had grown so bad she could not walk. the long journey, made more unbearable by the roundabout route they took to dissuade any attempts to rescue her, quickly sapped Mary's strength. The low, damp castle at Fotheringay received a tired, sick woman who would never again inspire men to her cause with her beauty and spirit. The fire within the Queen of Scots, dampened by years of imprisonment, had died that last day at Chartley. It was never to be rekindled.

Maria Elena Soledad Mendoza de Choulqueras was not pleased. On the contrary, she was bored to tears and extremely irritable. She was on her way to join her father, Don Luis Felipe de Choulqueras, Special Emissary of His Most Illustrous Majesty, Philip of Spain at the court of Elizabeth in England, but for two days the ship had been becalmed off the coast of Holland. To wile away the long hours, she had taken to walking on deck, despite the shocked protests of her duennas and the entreaties of her young maid, Ninetta, that she should not display herself before common seamen. She had paced the wooden decks until her feet ached, ignoring the sniggers and smiles from the sailors about her; after all, she was of noble birth and far too superior to allow herself to be disturbed by their crude remarks.

England seemed an eternity away. At her devotions only that morning she had prayed for a wind to speed the ship on its way, but still the sails remained slack. They were three days overdue. Her father would be growing anxious, and her future husband too. She had been led to believe he was of an impetuous nature. It was not likely he would take kindly to the marriage plans being delayed.

On her twentieth birthday, a few months before, Don Luis had proclaimed that on her wedding day his daughter would be the most beautiful woman at the English court. Hundreds of women slaves sewed day and night for three months to complete the wedding trousseau, and extra slaves were brought in from the coast of Peru to work in the Choulqueras silver mines, so that she would take with her a dowry large enough to make Elizabeth and all her courtiers gasp in wonder.

Maria Elena Choulqueras was indeed beautiful. She had the high cheekbones and delicately carved features hereditary in generations of Choulqueras and her father's colouring was predominant in the thick black hair swept high on to her head and surmounted by a jewelled comb. But here the resemblance ended. From an English mother, she had inherited a flawless skin as smooth and white as alabaster, and large green eyes which dominated the proud face.

From the tender age of five, she had been taught to obey her elders and submit herself to their domination without dispute. Over the past year she had known she was being carefully prepared for marriage and had accepted it as a natural event in her life. To marry and bear children were the main functions of a woman, or so she had been taught to believe. Love was unimportant and unnecessary. Obedience and submission to the man chosen to be her husband were the virtues of a good wife.

Sir Thomas Wyndham, her future husband, was little more than a name. Don Luis had told her he had vast estates in Cornwall and was twenty years her senior, but apart from that she knew nothing about him. Maria Elena had not commented on the difference in ages, but in her heart of hearts she had hoped to marry someone of her own age and for several days she had been utterly desolate. Then the strict years of discipline imposed on her triumphed and she had accepted her fate with the dignity becoming a Choulqueras. There was nothing else she could do.

"Sail – ho!"

She heard the lookout high above her cry out, but took no notice until sailors began leaving their posts to crowd the sides of the ship, pointing seawards and muttering in low undertones. Maria Elena mounted the stairs to the bridge where the captain stood, watching for the new arrival.

"Is it one of our ships?" she asked.

"My men are thinking it is the *Santa Margarita*, but I know she is at least three weeks behind us."

Maria Elena was alarmed to see beads of perspiration gathering on the man's thick brows.

"What ship is this, Captain Mendoza? Why are you afraid?"

"Afraid, Senorita? Ramon Alvares de Mendoza does not concern himself with his personal safety. My fears are for you. If that is the *Nemesis* behind us, you are in great danger."

"Nemesis, the Greek goddess of vengeance. What a strange name to use," Maria Elena murmured and shaded her eyes against the glare of the sun to stare with mounting interest at the second vessel.

"Not at all, the ship is aptly named. Its captain has sworn a terrible oath to exterminate the house of Choulqueras. For years he has destroyed our ships, after relieving them of their valuable cargoes. I was in an engagement with him last year. The man is a devil, invincible. I saw him wounded twice, yet still he fought with the strength of ten men."

Captain Mendoza grew pale at the remembrance of the encounter. He had lost thirty men and was in peril of losing the rest as well as his own life, when two ships of the Spanish navy cruising in that area had come upon them unexpectedly.

"Did he take your cargo too?" Maria Elena asked contemptuously. She had never heard of the *Nemesis* before, or its formidable captain, but she felt sure once he came close enough he would see that it was madness to attack a ship larger and more heavily armed than his own. She had been taught to despise weakness of any kind and was severely disciplined for the slightest lapse on her part, even though she was no longer a child and well on her way to being a bride. Her elder brother, Manuel, usually undertook the task of reprimanding her in a subtle manner that was excrutiatingly painful, yet left no marks on her body.

"May I suggest you go to your cabin?" Captain Mendoza said.

Maria Elena turned to watch the second ship coming up swiftly behind them.

"You may suggest it, Captain, but I have no intention of complying with your wishes. I am curious to see this invincible devil for myself."

"I am answerable to Don Luis for your safety," the captain protested.

"Then make sure he does not overtake us," Maria Elena replied softly.

The *San Cristobal*, the passenger ship conveying Maria Elena to England, was one of Luis Choulqueras' fastest ships, but like all Spanish vessels, it had the customary towering castles fore and aft and carried less sail than a man o' war. Before long it was obvious to everyone on deck that the *Nemesis* was closing rapidly.

The contemptuous mockery Maria Elena had displayed earlier faded as she took a spy-glass from the first officer beside her and looked at the monster ship for herself. It was a two-masted brigantine, considerably smaller than the *San Cristobal* and twice as fast. Its speed astounded her. Even as she studied it, figures on the deck became distinguishable. She saw a vividly painted figurehead of a woman and a little to the left of it, the clearly lettered name – *Nemesis*. For some unknown reason she shivered.

"What manner of crest is that on the sails?" she asked Ramon Mendoza.

The captain did not pause from issuing instructions to his officers to look at the insignia, he knew it only too well. A hand, cased in armour, resting on a coronet. The fingers clutched a cross.

"It is the badge of his clan, the MacDonalds. Faith, I'd rather face El Draco in battle than this accursed man. He will kill everyone aboard. He has never been known to give quarter. As for you, señorita—"

"Yes, Captain? What will he do with me?"

"I dread to think. If he does not cut your throat or give you to his crew after he has finished with you, he may hold you to ransom. Madre de Dios, he has no regard for womanhood, that one!"

"Should my sister ever fall into the hands of such a man she is fully aware of the one and only course to take," a sneering voice said close behind Maria Elena.

Instinctively she glanced down at the enormous emerald ring on her right hand, before looking up at her brother. Beneath the magnificent stone was enough deadly poison to kill her instantly. If this was taken from her, there was another in her jewel case. No man had ever laid hands on her in her life, save for her father and

Manuel, and none would until her husband laid claim to her. If she was dishonoured no man would want her and the disgrace brought upon the family name would be unbearable, therefore the only alternative was death. She had accepted this indoctrination along with the rest of her instruction and if the occasion arose, she knew that she would not hesitate to take her life.

"What is so special about this ship? The men are cringing like cowardly dogs."

Manuel Ruy de Choulqueras leaned over the rail, staring at the fast closing vessel, now not more than a mile from them. He had the same dark hair as his sister, but his skin was swarthy instead of fair and he was considerably taller and more heavily built.

"It is the *Nemesis*, señor," Captain Mendoza said. His agitation was increasing. If anything happened to his precious passengers his head would be forfeit, always provided he lived to face their illustrious father.

Manuel Choulqueras swore and regardless of his sister's disapproving frown, he repeated the oath with unconcealed vehemence.

"Adam MacDonald! I thought he was dead."

"He is a man with many lives," Captain Mendoza replied, tight-lipped.

"Do you know him?" Maria Elena asked her brother.

"Of course I know the murdering pirate. He bears the mark of my dagger on his face. Give me that glass." Manuel snatched it from her hand and turned it on the *Nemesis*. "Mother of God, he still lives! Look, little sister, and see the face of the devil himself."

Maria Elena stooped beneath his arm and peered through the glass trained on a man in the bows, his arms folded over the leather bandolier across his chest. He stood tall and arrogant, shouting orders to the crew scurrying on the lower decks. She glimpsed a hard brown face turned in the direction of the *San Cristobal* before Manuel jerked the glass away

"If he overtakes us and we are taken, you will not become his prisoner. Do I make myself clear?"

Maria Elena nodded, casting a worried glance at the *Nemesis*.

"But, he won't catch us, will he?"

"Go down on your knees and pray he does not, for all our sakes."

Maria Elena could not drag her horrified gaze from the enemy ship which was drawing closer every second. Her lips trembled as her fingers touched the emerald ring. She would obey her brother if the worst happened, rather than fall into the hands of this pirate captain and be subjected to heaven knew what indignities.

"She's falling back," Manuel muttered. "Madre de Dios, what game is that son of Satan playing now?"

"Perhaps he is afraid, we are bigger," she began.

"Be quiet, you foolish child, you talk nonsense," her brother snapped. 'He is afraid of nothing on this earth. It would seem he plays cat and mouse to unnerve us."

Far above them the lookout's cry broke across his voice.

"Sail on the starboard bow."

Captain Mendoza muttered a frenzied oath and swung about and then Maria Elena saw relief spring to his face.

"It flies an English flag. It is the *Revenge*, El Draco's ship."

"Our escort vessel," Manuel said, and his face broke into a broad smile. "The English queen has great respect for our father to send the great Francis Drake to watch over us." He looked down into his sister's flushed cheeks. "The excitement is past, I suggest you go to your cabin and prepare yourself for our arrival. With a good wind we shall reach Tilbury by tomorrow night."

"You do not think this Adam MacDonald will try to attack us now?" she ventured to ask.

"Under the guns of El Draco – never! MacDonald is no fool. You have had a lucky escape, sister, you would not have enjoyed meeting Adam MacDonald, believe me. His reputation with women leaves much to be desired."

Under the surveillance of the *Revenge*, the Spanish galleon sailed into Tilbury without further hindrance. The brigantine, *Nemesis* remained some miles to their rear, but always in sight until they came in view of the Dover cliffs and then it suddenly dropped behind the horizon and was not seen again. Manuel Choulqueras' comments were most scathing that evening, when he and Maria Elena entertained Sir Francis Drake to dinner in the captain's cabin. His guest said very little on the subject.

In his forty-third year Francis Drake, eldest son of a yeoman farmer, was an impressive figure of a man. He had lost his slimness of youth and was now inclined to be a little on the portly side, but this was exonerated by his grandeur of bearing. He had a proud, weatherbeaten face, graced by a small moustache and a neat little beard trimmed to perfection. At sea or on land, his taste in clothes was always impeccable. He did not care for Manuel Choulqueras, but was aware both he and his sister had been afforded the protection of the Queen and were therefore her honoured guests. He had dressed accordingly in his best sacque coat of rich blue silk with the slashed sleeves picked out in cloth of gold and breeches of dark blue velvet.

Clothes had been rich and colourful during the reign of Henry VIII, and with Elizabeth's reign they grew even more so. Silks and beautiful velvet cloth was brought from across the Channel. The rich set the fashion for the remainder of the people and at the court of the Queen of England, fashion was at its height, although no one had been able to match the glitter and splendour of Elizabeth herself.

During the course of the evening, Drake often found himself admiring the exquisite little figure seated opposite him, jewels flashing at her throat and wrists, the golden threads of her gown shimmering in the candlelight. Thomas Wyndham was lucky to be marrying such a beautiful girl; it was a pity she would never be appreciated. Drake knew she was to be used as a pawn in a deadly war being waged at court between the supporters of Elizabeth on one side and Mary Stuart on the other. It was only too clear how Thomas Wyndham would profit by the alliance, but exactly what Luis Choulqueras would gain from it he did not know, and it worried him.

"I don't believe you have been to England before?" he said to his hostess.

Maria Elena smiled shyly. She had naturally heard stories of the famous "El Draco" and had been expecting a monster with six heads who breathed fire. Instead she discovered a courteous, quietly spoken man whose charming personality soon put her at her ease. Six heads indeed!

"No, Señor Drake, I have never been away from Spain before." She laughed softly. "*Por favor*, you must forgive my bad English. My brother tells me as I am soon to marry an Englishman, I must grow accustomed to his tongue. I find it most strange."

"You are too modest, Señorita Choulqueras," Drake said graciously. "I can understand you perfectly and the accent is quite charming. You will capture the hearts of everyone at court, including Sir Thomas."

Maria Elena blushed and lowered her eyes. The voyage was almost over and soon she would be meeting her future husband. Why was she not pleased at the prospect of their first encounter? She caught sight of Manuel frowning in her direction and quickly returned her attention to their guest. He had already reprimanded her once that day for not remaining long enough at her prayers. Her left arm still ached where he had twisted it behind her back.

Manuel was her father's right hand, he could do no wrong and her father was in full agreement that she should be disciplined from time to time lest she forgot she was only a weak-willed woman – a servant of men. Her brother possessed no English strain. His mother had been Don Luis' mistress, who had died shortly after the birth. It was rumoured that she was the only woman he had ever loved. Why else had he chosen to acknowledge an illegitimate son?

The pure Spanish blood of the Choulqueras mingled with the fire of a *gitana* girl flowed through Manuel's veins. His temper was quick and often violent and he had a streak of meanness in him which made servants cower back in terror whenever he passed by, lest they be chosen to provide his sport that day.

Maria Elena was his chief victim, mainly because he had hated the pale-faced Englishwoman who had become his step-mother. He had never accepted her and after her death, he took pleasure in tormenting the beautiful girl she had left behind.

"More wine, Captain Drake?" Maria Elena asked.

"Thank you, no. I regret it is time I took my leave." Francis Drake rose to his feet with an apologetic smile. "The carriage will be here to take you to London at nine o'clock. I trust that is not too early?"

"My sister is eager to be with Sir Thomas," Manuel said dryly. "Escort our guest to the upper deck, Maria Elena." He leaned back in his chair, making no move to rise and accompany them, and refilled his empty wine goblet, totally ignoring Drake's outstretched hand.

Francis Drake's mouth tightened angrily. He bowed shortly and followed his hostess up on to the upper deck where a pleasant night breeze quickly dispelled the rage mounting inside him. Maria Elena looked up at him hesitantly.

"Please, forgive my brother. It has been a long journey and we are both anxious to be on dry land again and with our father. Manuel is tired. . . ."

"I understand, believe me," Drake said quietly.

He cared less for Manuel Choulqueras than he did his father. They were Spaniards and Papists and he hated both. His own father and family had been cruelly persecuted during the reign of "Bloody Mary" and many friends and relatives had died for their Protestant faith. He found himself wishing that the *Nemesis* had overtaken the Choulqueras ship before he arrived and saved him the distasteful task of escorting the beautiful girl beside him to a disastrous marriage alliance and the equally unpleasant hours he would be forced to spend in the company of her odious brother.

"May I ask you a question, Captain Drake?"

"Of course."

"Do all the English hate my people?"

Drake looked down into her enquiring eyes with a frown. She was far more perceptive than he had realised.

"Some have good reason, as you are no doubt aware."

"Have you?"

"Yes."

"I believe you, and I will not ask why." She smiled briefly. "A woman is not supposed to concern herself with such matters, but I would like to look on you as a friend, Captain Drake. Is that too much to ask?"

Drake bent low over her outstretched hand and touched the slender fingers to his lips.

"No, it is very little."

"As a friend, will you always be truthful with me?"

"I am not a man given to lying," Drake answered with a sudden hardening of tone.

Maria Elena stared at him intently.

"Tell me then of this Captain MacDonald. Why did his ship follow us all the way to the English coast?"

"As a friend I can only tell you that Adam MacDonald is dangerous. I pray to God you'll never have the misfortune to meet him."

"Perhaps the stories of him are exaggerated as were those I heard of you?"

"Whatever you hear – believe."

"You seem very sure, Captain Drake."

"I have good reason. Adam MacDonald and I have been friends since childhood. Goodnight, Señorita Choulqueras."

Francis Drake bowed low before her and turned away before she could question him further.

Maria Elena returned to the captain's cabin where she found Manuel still drinking heavily. During the short time she had been absent, he had managed to get through half a bottle of wine.

"Captain Drake has gone, Manuel."

Her brother raised his head and stared at her sullenly. His face was flushed his eyes already bloodshot and the hand holding the solid gold goblet was shaking so much that spots of blood-red wine spilled down the front of his doublet. When he was drunk he was unbelievably cruel. Maria Elena quickly took out her lace handkerchief and moved around the table towards him, praying that she could persuade him to stop before the intoxicating wine awakened in him the sadistic bully she feared so greatly.

"Let me," she began, but her hand was knocked roughly aside.

"Pour me more wine and then go to your cabin. I shall be along later to hear you at your devotions."

"Oh, no, Manuel, I swear I will remember everything you have told me. With the guidance of the Blessed Virgin I shall be a good wife and mother."

"This marriage is of great importance to Father's plans, Maria Elena. One wrong word or the slightest shudder of distaste when Wyndham touches you could result in disaster. Before you meet your future husband tomorrow, I must make sure you are fully aware of my feelings in this matter."

His sister paled visibly.

"You told me Sir Thomas was young for his forty years and handsome too. Have you lied to me?"

"You have been told all you need to know. Tomorrow you will find out for yourself." Manuel's dark eyes slowly roved over her slim form. "He will have no cause to be dissatisfied. You are pretty enough despite the English blood in your veins, and you have been well schooled. But that foolish tongue, sister – you must learn to control it before it is too late. Go to your cabin and wait for me."

Maria Elena knew it was useless to argue further and risk his anger unnecessarily.

"Very well, Manuel," she said quietly, and left him.

After two long hours had elapsed and Manuel had not put in an appearance, Maria Elena decided he had drunk himself into a stupor and was not coming. Overwhelmed with relief she dismissed her young maid, finished her prayers and climbed into bed. She was half asleep by the time her brother blundered into the room, cursing vehemently as he fell over a trunk.

"Maria Elena, I told you to wait for me. Damn you, I'll teach you to disobey me."

She cried out in pain as he grabbed a handful of her loose hair and pulled her bodily from the bed.

"I'm sorry, Manuel—"

Her pleas died away at the sight of his furious features. What she feared had happened; he was drunk and feeling violent, and as usual she was to be his whipping post.

"I must break this rebellious spirit of yours, sister, before you give Sir Thomas cause to complain."

His eyes glittered maliciously at the terror in her eyes as he reached down for her. Nothing gave him greater pleasure, except perhaps the thought of his sweet, virginal little sister being married to and mastered by a lecherous old man of twice her age.

The brigantine *Nemesis* lay at anchor in one of the many hidden coves lining the Cornish coast. Its crew, with the exception of the sailors left on board on watch, were celebrating the return to land in the local village tavern.

They were always welcome for they brought goods to trade and sell, mostly their shares from looted Spanish ships, and their pockets overflowed with money.

Adam MacDonald paid wages far in excess of the ten shillings a month paid to ordinary seamen, and each of his crew received a share of booty from any captured ships. In return he demanded complete loyalty from those who sailed with him and gave no quarter to anyone who ran foul of his laws. Of the few foolish or discontented enough to risk his anger, none had lived to boast of it.

"Capt'n, Paco says he's got your horse waiting in the yard." Abel Black, first mate of the *Nemesis* stood looking down at the man sipping a tankard of Malmsey ale. In one hairy hand he held a jug himself, while the other was clasped around the waist of a buxom village girl. "Are ye not staying wi' us?"

"No, Abel, I have business in London."

"One of them court wenches, eh? What's wrong wi' the likes of Jenny here?"

Adam MacDonald slowly uncoiled himself from his chair. He was as agile as a mountain cat despite his height and build, as many men had discovered to their cost. A smile touched his lean mouth.

"If my business was not important, my friend, I might feel inclined to take her from you," he returned amusedly. "As it is, I must leave you to make sure the men don't tear the place apart, and give them a warning from me. If I find any of them laying hands on an unwilling woman, they'll answer to me personally. Do I make myself clear?"

"All women are unwilling at first, Capt'n, it's their way," Abel grinned. There was no answering smile on his captain's face and he nodded agreement. "They'll behave themselves. Capt'n, was there a rich haul on the *San Cristobal*?"

"There was indeed and but for Drake, we'd have had her."

"What was it. Cargo – jewels?"

A strange look entered Adam MacDonald's eyes.

"None of those, Abel, but believe me, it was worth having. To me it was priceless. Give the men their fill of drink and women and get them back on board in time to reach your anchorage tomorrow night. I'll see you then."

The girl beside Abel Black stared after his departing figure, her eyes wide with surprise.

"What's more important than jewels?" she asked.

"That, my wench, depends on how much you hate a certain Spaniard by the name of Don Luis Choulqueras."

Adam MacDonald arrived in London as it was growing light. Through deserted streets where early mists still lingered, he rode to his town house situated in a quiet cul-de-sac near St. James's.

A yawning servant girl was leaning out of an upstairs window staring dubiously at the cloudy sky as he turned into the small cobbled courtyard. She glanced down, her mouth gaped still more and immediately she disappeared from view.

A moment later a kilted figure came out through the main doorway and leapt down the steps to embrace the younger man.

"Jamie – man, it's good to see you." Adam disengaged himself from the bear-hug and smiled into the bearded face before him.

Jamie MacDonald had been his father's steward for twenty-five years and had remained after his death to guard and minister to the young laird he had raised from boyhood.

"Ye are alive, I knew it." There were tears in the old man's eyes. "I wouldna' believe ye had died at the hands of that filthy Spaniard."

"Did you not get my message?"

"Nay, nothing, but 'tis not important now. Into the house wi' ye. Have ye had a long ride?"

"Aye, from the coast," Adam answered.

He strode into the house, tossing his cloak and gloves down on to the table in the main hall and continued on to his study. The interior of the room was typical of others throughout the house. Huge colourful tapestries depicting hunting scenes with horsemen, dogs and boars or fleeing stags, hung from the walls. The high-backed chairs and the couch were covered in crimson velvet cloth to match the window drapes and there was even a carpet, an item which denoted position and wealth in those days.

"Sit ye down and have a dram," Jamie said. "I've sent a servant to prepare yer rooms. Ye'll be needing some sleep."

"In a while, old friend, I have a letter to write first." Adam relaxed down into his favourite chair and stretched his long legs towards the empty hearth. He took the glass his steward held out to him with a slow smile. "Highland whisky, now I know I'm home."

"Since when have ye looked on this place as home?" Jamie returned dourly. "It's nary more than a convenience – a place to stay when ye are on dry land."

Adam's gaze wandered over the rich tapestries and antique furniture and knew it was the truth. He had bought this house and furnished it without caring for the cost so that he would always have a quiet retreat when a voyage was over, yet somehow the comfort and luxury of his surroundings meant nothing to him. He had never been able to relax here – to forget his sworn vows of vengeance until he sailed again. He had lost count of the many women who had come and gone from his bed and still the empty feeling remained.

Jamie felt a moment of apprehension as Adam looked up at him. They had not seen each other for over a year and in that time the expression in the young man's eyes had grown still colder, more pitiless. It was like looking into the eyes of death.

"Until Don Luis and his pup are dead, I'll have neither home nor peace of mind," Adam said in a low tone. "Now, leave the bottle and ring for a messenger to take a letter to the Queen. She must grant me an audience before the day is out. I have news to interest her and our friend Francis Drake."

The steward's face registered disgust as he obeyed.

"Ye owe no allegiance to the English," he muttered. "A King in petticoats."

"I've not heard you speak thus of her cousin Mary."

"At least she's a Catholic."

Adam rose to his feet and crossed to the writing bureau against the far wall, a deep frown furrowing his brows. With Mary practically under sentence of death, anyone who spoke her name above a whisper was in danger of being labelled a Papist and faced, not only imprisonment, but a similar fate. Jamie MacDonald was a Scot and a Catholic and proud of both. Adam shared his pride of heritage, but cared little for God, or who sat on the throne of England, so long as he was left alone to pursue his vendetta against the house of Choulqueras. Religion had not mattered to him for many years, not since he had knelt beside his dying father on the deck of their shattered ship and begged God for his life. Michael MacDonald had died and with him, Adam's ability to believe. He sat down, took out writing materials and began his letter.

"You'd best curb that tongue, Jamie, or you'll find yourself on the rack," he said without looking up.

He wrote steadily for a few moments, then sealed the letter with the gold crested ring on his left hand and gave it to the waiting messenger with instructions to deliver it personally to the Queen, then he went to bed.

It was strange to awaken that afternoon to the sound of street cries from outside the window, instead of the sound of waves lapping against the bows of the *Nemesis*. As he lay staring at the room he realised that Jamie had been right. The house was not a home, merely a refuge, and after a few days he would tire of being on dry land and become bored by the life at court, longing instead for the feel of a crisp breeze on his face. But this time he would not be able to give way to his desire to return to sea. Not only was Don Luis in London, but Manuel also and the daughter Adam knew of by reputation only. He cursed the ill luck that had prevented him from overtaking the *San Cristobal* before Drake's ship arrived on the scene.

Damn Drake, Adam thought without malice. If they had not been such close friends he would have blown him out of the water for his inopportune arrival. As it was they would meet at the palace and probably spend a pleasant evening together getting drunk. Afterwards he would seek out his mistress, the Lady Caroline Stacey, one of the Queen's ladies-in-waiting. After five long months at sea he was hungry for the company of a beautiful woman. His quarry would not disappear overnight, and it would give him the chance to catch up on the latest gossip. Caroline's position near the Queen made her an invaluable source of information.

He had washed and dressed and was on his way downstairs when Jamie came out into the hall, holding a letter.

"Is that my answer?" Adam demanded.

"Aye, it's just come."

Adam took it from him and strode into the drawing-room, breaking the seal as he went. The steward followed and stood in silence while his master read the letter. His eyes flickered upwards to the portrait hanging on the wall directly behind Adam. It was of Michael MacDonald, painted when he was thirty. Father and son might have been twins. There were the same handsome features, the thick black hair and dark piercing eyes. There was even the same arrogance in the thrown-back head and stance as Adam looked up.

"I've an audience with the Queen this evening," he said quietly. "Also an invitation to supper."

"It will be best if ye return to the house directly after ye have seen her. The streets will not be safe for the likes of us tonight."

"You talk in riddles, man."

"Anthony Babington is to be executed at Lincoln's Inn at noon today."

Adam went white. They had been drinking friends for several years. He both liked and respected the young boy despite his ardent Papist zeal and for a moment the news stunned him.

"Ye have chosen an ill time to come back," Jamie continued. "There was a plot to murder the English Queen and free her cousin, but it misfired. Anthony and a man called Ballard were arrested and that officer, Savage. Ye ken Savage, ye played cards together here in this very room?"

"I remember him. Are they all to die?"

Jamie nodded, not flinching as Adam turned suspicious eyes in his direction.

"Were you part of it?"

"I kept their secret, it was the least I could do, and I hid young Babington, before his arrest, in this house."

"Are you out of your tired old mind?" Adam stepped towards him, his face tightening angrily. "If any of them talk, you will have your neck stretched too, not to mention the fact I shall be implicated."

"Some of us still remember the religion of our fathers," Jamie MacDonald answered with dignity. "I'll have some food prepared for ye, if ye still have the stomach for it." He bowed stiffly before Adam's furious features and walked out of the room.

Adam swore after his departing figure and poured himself a large glass of whisky from the bottle on the table beside him. He rarely ate before evening when on dry land and had made it a habit to consume a large amount of liquor instead, which would have completely intoxicated a lesser man.

Damn Jamie MacDonald's stubborn Scots pride, he thought worriedly. It was time he realised Mary Stuart would never sit on the throne of England.

CHAPTER TWO

"THE man's a rogue," Elizabeth declared fiercely. Then the anger vanished from her face and she sat back in her chair and began to laugh. "If only I could have seen his face when you sailed into his sights, and yours, my dear Francis!"

Francis Drake turned from the window to look at the figure in the chair, resplendent in brilliant blue satin and velvet, with sapphires flashing on her wrists and in her hair. Gradually his tight features broke into a smile.

"I'm glad Your Majesty finds the situation amusing. Rogue or not, Adam MacDonald is my friend and it would have grieved me to kill him to defend Don Luis Choulqueras' kin."

Annoyance flashed through Elizabeth's brown eyes.

"You were obeying your Queen." She rose to her feet and stood watching him through narrowed eyes. Friends for a queen were few and far between; Elizabeth had learned to do without them at an early age. On many occasions she displayed a lack of feeling characteristic of the Tudors, on others, the temper and vanity of her beautiful, tragic mother, Anne Boleyn. She was masculine in coarseness of words and actions when the demand arose, and yet the very same people who had fled from her presence in terror one day were back in court the next, being soothed by the charm she had inherited from her father, Henry VIII.

Adam MacDonald was shown into the Queen's private sitting-room an hour later. Elizabeth waved Francis

Drake to remain seated, her gaze fixed steadily on the tall figure that swept down before her.

"Have you taken leave of your senses?" she demanded in a fierce whisper, and her eyes were centred on the red and green plaid hanging from his shoulder as she spoke. "First you attack the *San Cristobal* and now you parade through the streets in – in that attire. You have been away a long time, Captain MacDonald; perhaps I should acquaint you with what has been happening."

"I came here by way of Lincoln's Inn, madam," Adam returned dryly. "I was raised a Catholic as my father before me and I've never pretended otherwise – I'm not ashamed of it, although I haven't practised my religion since the age of sixteen. I have no faith in God, nor man, only in the strength of my sword arm. However I am still a MacDonald and proud of it. I'd rather you banished me from court than forbade me to wear the plaid."

"There are those who would like to see me do both," Elizabeth answered quickly, "but the time has not yet come when I heed the prattle of idle tongues. You have served me well, Adam MacDonald, as your father did, despite your inability to see when a ship is flying my personal pennant. In Spanish waters you may do what you please, but here Don Luis has a pledge of safe-conduct. Do not make the same mistake again or your head will be forfeit."

Adam bowed respectfully. Only Drake saw the mocking gleam in his eyes, which vanished as quickly as it came.

"I rarely make the same mistake twice, madam. Rest assured, I'll never cause you another moment's embarrassment."

The audience lasted until the first of the guests began to arrive. Francis Drake drew Adam to one side as they entered the supper room.

"Are you sure of the number of ships you saw at Cadiz?"

"I'm not likely to forget, I lost two good men to get the information. Philip is planning an invasion, and if I'm not mistaken Don Luis is up to his scrawny neck in the plot."

Francis thought of the forthcoming marriage between Maria Elena Choulqueras and Sir Thomas Wyndham and nodded gravely.

"I'm afraid you're right," he said and explained the reason he had escorted the *San Cristobal* to England. He watched his friend's face for some sign which would betray why he had returned home so unexpectedly, but Adam's dark features were unreadable. "What are you up to, my friend?" he asked when it became obvious the information was not going to be volunteered.

"Was I up to anything?" Adam's amused eyes met those of Francis Drake over the rim of his tankard. "You have a suspicious nature."

"When I arrived, the *Nemesis* was closing with Mendoza's ship and you weren't doing it merely to wish him a safe journey. Did you not see the ship was flying the Queen's pennant? Had you opened fire, I'd have been forced to blow you out of the water. You'd be dead by now or in the Tower."

"Or in possession of a very precious cargo," Adam added softly.

"By all the saints, you knew Don Luis' daughter was aboard! I always said you were a pirate," Drake declared.

"Which is why we get on so well together," came the infuriating retort. "Not even El Draco's great guns will keep me from my revenge. The next time we meet, I won't turn my ship aside."

"That will be most regrettable, old friend." Drake stared at the hard brown face before him with sympathetic eyes. "I know how you feel, believe me. I hate the Don too, but this is neither the time nor place to force a showdown. London is a seething cauldron of hate which could boil over at any moment. To force the Don into a fight will provoke the Queen's anger. You'll achieve nought by doing that and you may lose your head."

"At least I'd have had the satisfaction of bringing Luis Choulqueras and his bastard son to account for their crimes." Adam's voice was cold and his face had lost its smile.

"Be sensible, lad. With what crimes can you charge them?"

"The abduction of my mother ten years ago. The burning of our home. The murder of my father. Shall I go on?"

"Your mother went of her own free will and well you know it. As for your father, he died in a battle at sea. You would do well to consider your position here, my foolish young friend. You're a Scot, and to most people at the moment that means only one thing – a Catholic ready to hatch some plot against the Queen. Provoke the Spaniard too far and you'll find yourself in the Tower for some considerable time. The Queen dares not risk any unpleasantness with Mary's trial about to take place. Go back to the *Nemesis*, Adam, and wait for Don Luis at sea."

Adam leaned back against the tapestry-covered wall and smiled. It was not a pleasant smile and Drake inwardly winced. He could talk until he was blue about the gills and it would be useless. Adam MacDonald was hell bent on the road of revenge and nothing could stop him. His hate was all-consuming and he feared neither man nor Queen.

Drake quickly finished his wine and took Adam's empty tankard.

"Let me get you another," he said. "We came here to enjoy ourselves, not discuss the uncertainty of your future."

As he moved away, Adam's eyes slowly roved over the sea of faces around him and he found himself wondering where Caroline Stacey was. If she did not appear soon, he would go to her apartments. These supper parties invariably bored him after a few hours and had it not been for the pleasure of seeing Don Luis' face when they encountered each other, he would have gone straight back to the house.

Something in green moving across the far end of the room arrested his attention and he found himself looking at one of the most beautiful women he had ever seen. Slim and exquisitely dressed, she had a poise and elegance which set her apart from the other women in the room. Adam knew at once she was not English. The gown she wore betrayed her, for it was slashed straight across her breasts, without the huge lace ruff and trimmings the Queen herself had set in fashion. Jewels flashed on the unknown girl's wrists and throat, as magnificent as those of the Queen of England at whose side she stood. All thought of Caroline vanished from Adam's mind.

He waited impatiently for Francis Drake to return.

"Who is that beautiful girl?"

Drake followed his gaze and frowned heavily.

"Of all women you should know her name," he said meaningly.

Adam's eyes glittered with surprise. He had not expected anyone so utterly captivating.

"It can't be. She's far too lovely to be his daughter."

"She is, and I advise you to keep your distance. Don't start trouble tonight."

"Trouble – I?" Adam's gaze was intent on the raven-haired girl with the face of an angel, now only a few yards from them. Now that the shock had passed he was angry with himself for not noticing the family resemblance. He hated this girl because of the accursed name she bore, and the momentary attraction vanished abruptly.

"Introduce me," he murmured.

"I'm damned if I will," Drake swore. He was not sure of Adam's intentions and it worried him.

"If you wish me to behave myself for the rest of the evening, do as I ask," Adam said and began moving slowly in the direction of Maria Elena. He neatly positioned himself behind her, so that when she turned, it was impossible not to collide with him.

"How clumsy of me. Please excuse me."

The quiet, attractive voice made no mark on Adam's already calculating mind. Providence had provided him with a weapon against his enemy and he intended to make good use of her, regardless of opposition from Francis Drake or the Queen herself.

"You must forgive my companion, he has a habit of getting in the way of beautiful women." Drake moved quickly forward, hiding his annoyance at Adam's action. He had warned the girl about him, yet here he was about to introduce them to each other. God forbid! "May I present an old friend, Captain Adam MacDonald? The lady is Don Luis' daughter, Adam, as you already know. She has come to England to be married."

Maria Elena grew very pale. She stared at Francis Drake as if he had introduced the devil himself, then slowly her eyes came to rest on the handsome man before her. Was it possible? Was this the man her father and brother had sworn must die? Yes, it was him, although the brief glance she had had of him from the deck of the *San Cristobal* had been deceptive. He was taller and his skin far darker, and for the first time she saw the thin, white scar on his left cheek. Her brother had done that, and no doubt he had derived great pleasure from it.

While she stood speechless, Adam reached out and raised her fingers to his lips.

"You are to marry Sir Thomas Wyndham, I believe." Derisive mockery burned in his eyes. "May I offer my – condolences?"

Maria Elena gasped in horror and tore her hand free, fierce colour flooding into her cheeks. She turned appealingly to Francis Drake.

"Captain Drake, I must protest."

"Every man is entitled to his own opinion," Adam murmured. "This is still a free country, not yet under Philip's Papist thumb, and you'll do well to remember it. Spaniards belong in Spain. Why don't you go home and take the rest of your brood with you?"

Francis Drake opened his mouth to intervene, but then he caught sight of Maria Elena's face and said nothing. The surprise had disappeared and in its place was an expression of utter contempt. Fierce anger burned in the depths of her green eyes – magnificent, like green fire. Adam would not score the victory he had hoped for her.

"I have heard of you, Captain MacDonald. Your reputation and your manners leave much to be desired," she said, and there was contempt in her voice too.

It made no impression on Adam. He was merely relieved that she had not dissolved into tears at their first encounter

A few yards away a distinguished-looking man stared across at the trio and immediately excused himself from his companions. He nudged the elbow of a younger man standing nearby and next moment Luis Choulqueras and his son Manuel appeared on either side of Maria Elena.

"You are ignoring our friends," Manuel growled to his sister, glaring with unconcealed vehemence at Adam and Drake. "Thomas would not like to see you in the company of this Englishman. I have warned you about him."

"I'm a Scot, with a long memory," Adam interrupted softly, and his fingers touched his scarred cheek for a brief moment. "Heed your brother, señorita, our next meeting may be even less to your liking."

"If you dare to lay a finger on her—"

"*Silencio*, Manuel," Don Luis said sharply. "Captain MacDonald is not a fool. If he wishes to harm any of us, he will choose a time and place far less conspicuous. I thought I had killed you," he said turning to Adam. His voice was so void of emotion he might have been discussing the weather.

He had long since learned not to be angered by this extremely irritating young pup whose mother he had seduced and taken back to Spain and discarded when her usefulness was over. Sarah MacDonald had been a beautiful woman, bored with her husband and begging for a lover, but she had been too demanding, too clinging, until at last he, Luis Choulqueras, had found it necessary and infinitely relieving to dispense with her services. He had found a replacement by that time anyway. She had died of a fever in some pest-ridden hole on the waterfront, so he had been told. He had never bothered to make enquiries. Alive she had been an embarrassment – he preferred her dead.

"I don't die easily."

"So I have discovered in the past. When my daughter's wedding is over, I shall accommodate you more successfully."

"Why wait, Father?" Manuel's hand was on his sword. The scar on Adam's face mocked him, a constant reminder how difficult it was to kill this man. He had failed twice, and his father was talking of giving the assignment to professional assassins.

"Tell your son that if he shows an inch of blade, he'll have a scar to match mine, Don Luis," Adam hissed and they all saw he had a slim-bladed dirk in the palm of his right hand, half-hidden by the lace ruffles of his sleeve. Only Drake knew it had come from the sheath strapped to his arm. Adam went nowhere without it, or the twin, hidden in his stocking. At sea, the latter would nestle just inside his sea-boot, quickly accessible and deadly.

"You forget yourself, Captain MacDonald. How dare you draw a weapon in the Queen's presence?" Drake's voice was cold with anger and there was no friendliness in the eyes which fixed themselves on the younger man. The hot-headed fool had gone too far this time. "I suggest you take a walk in the gardens until your temper has cooled."

Adam smiled. If he was annoyed it did not show. Maria Elena uttered a thankful prayer under her breath as the knife disappeared from sight, and she released her apprehensive hold on her father's arm.

"You're right, this is neither the time nor place. Look to my back, Francis," he said sardonically and walked away.

"Father, let me . . ." Manuel started forward.

"Escort your sister to Sir Thomas," Don Luis ordered curtly.

He was exceedingly pale and breathing heavily. Only Drake's presence forbade him sending his son after their enemy and disposing of him for all time. Father and son glared at each other and then Manuel seized Maria Elena painfully by the wrist and led her away.

"Manuel, let go. You are hurting me."

"Be glad I do not have the time to punish you for consorting with thieves and pirates."

"Captain Drake introduced us, it would have been rude to ignore them."

"Rude!" Manuel looked as if he might hit her despite the people milling around them. "No doubt if he had invited you to take the air, you would have gone with him and allowed yourself to be seduced."

"Manuel – no."

"You stupid little fool, you don't think he was interested in meeting you, do you? He only wanted to engage you in conversation until we saw you together. He wants a fight, and by the Holy Mother I'll give him one before I'm through."

"Is he so very dangerous?" Maria Elena ventured to ask. For all his rudeness she found it hard to believe that Adam MacDonald was a ruthless killer. He was too handsome – too well-spoken to be a common pirate. He just did not have the look of a murderer, although it was possible had she been taken to Newgate Prison and confronted with a dozen of London's worst criminals, she would not have thought them dangerous either. Her strictly guarded circle of acquaintances comprised of her immediate family, her duennas and her faithful Ninetta, who watched over her wherever she went. Never before had she known the freedom she was now experiencing at the English court, and she had yet to learn not to take people at face value.

Her question did not improve Manuel's temper. He led her to a fairly quiet spot in the room and pushed her down into a chair with an oath.

"Adam MacDonald is the murderous son of a Scots pig. He raids our galleons and takes the lives of our sailors without quarter and eludes capture with the luck of the devil. I have lost count of how many men he has killed and how many women he has seduced along the coast of Cartagena."

"But—"

"No buts, sister. If he attempts to converse with you again, call the guard and have him arrested for molesting you. Sir Thomas is a jealous man, he would not like to find out that his future bride has been touched by another." Manuel straightened, his eyes glittering maliciously. "Here comes your betrothed now. Pray he did not see you together."

Maria Elena's relief was overwhelming when it became obvious that Sir Thomas Wyndham had not been present in the room during the unpleasant encounter. She was still deeply upset at the deception practised on her which gave her in marriage to a fat, unpleasant man over twice her age. Had he begun to remonstrate with her, she knew she would burst into tears.

Her arrival in London had not been as successful as she had hoped. The coach ride from Tilbury, over rough roads had jarred every bone in her body and all attempts at conversation had been thwarted by Manuel. She was still in disgrace in his eyes and therefore allowed no privileges. The journey was the most miserable she had ever endured in her life, but far worse was to follow. The streets had been crowded with people waving flags and banners, the words of which seared her vision. "England for the Protestants" – "Death to Mary" – "Burn Mary".

Her horrified protests to Francis Drake had met with a cold, polite denial of what was happening. It had been a relief to arrive at the palace at Westminster and go to her apartments. She had had only a few hours before the start of the huge supper ball in her honour. Manuel's parting shot warned her to take great care with her appearance. Her father did not deem it necessary to welcome his daughter. Maria Elena would have been very surprised if he had.

Her entrance to the Supper Room had caused a stir. She had looked magnificent in a gown of rich green velvet, adorned with countless diamonds and pearls and her mother's emeralds around her throat. Even her father had complimented her on her appearance as he led her towards the Queen.

Maria Elena had searched the room in vain for a man who might resemble her future husband, and by the time Don Luis led her to a small antechamber to show her off to her betrothed, she had been in a state of nerves.

Twenty years her senior but fair of face and elegant, a man of looks and breeding, Manuel had told her. The man whose pale eyes scrutinised her could easily have been three score years. The brown hair with its reddish tints was obviously dyed and styled to suit a far younger man, as were the extravagant clothes – the large rings flashing on thick, short fingers. He was barely as tall as Maria Elena and fat, not plump, although the cut of his satin doublet was meant to hide the fact better than it did. She had stood silent, horrified while he took her hand in his and raised it to his mouth. His touch had made her shudder. How would she endure the years ahead when she must submit to his every wish? Surely God could not be cruel enough to watch her marry this revolting creature!

"My dear girl, are you not well?" Thomas was peering down into her face now, a hot, podgy hand was pressing hers. Slight as the pressure was, she felt instant revulsion. Over his shoulder, she saw Manuel smiling. How he must hate her to have deceived her so!

"I am a little tired, Sir Thomas," she said bravely.

"It is a pleasant night," Manuel murmured meaningly. "The fresh air will no doubt revive her."

Thomas Wyndham's pale eyes lit up. He had not been alone yet with this exciting creature. She was soon to be his wife, so he was allowed some liberties.

"An excellent idea. Come, my dear, take my arm."

Maria Elena cast an appealing glance at her brother, but it was ignored. Wearily she rose to her feet, dropping her fan as she did so. Manuel handed it back to her, leaning close, his lips against her ear.

"Be pleasant to him, little sister, he is an important ally. If he is displeased with you—"

He left the sentence unfinished and walked away, leaving his sister trembling with horror. Was she to allow herself to be pawed by the oversized excuse for a man even before the hateful marriage took place?

She closed her eyes and did indeed begin to feel unwell. She allowed herself to be escorted out of the stuffy Supper Room into the still, coolness of the night air. Apart from a few couples admiring the well-laid-out gardens, Maria Elena found herself alone with her future husband.

"Are you feeling better now?" Thomas Wyndham enquired as they moved slowly down a moonlit path towards a tiny waterfall set in a rockery some yards away.

Maria Elena gave an apprehensive little smile.

"The air is most refreshing. You are most kind, Sir Thomas, but I do not wish to drag you away from your friends."

"My friends can go to hell," Thomas said hoarsely.

They were well away from the balustrade by now. He halted, gazing down into the lovely face beside him. In the moonlight her skin was like alabaster. Don Luis had not overstressed her charms. Thomas' eyes became fixed on the firm swelling breasts above the neckline of her gown and his mouth went dry. It was impossible to wait until their wedding night. He was not used to restraining his sensual appetite where women were concerned, and as

Maria Elena would soon belong to him anyway he was stupid to prolong the inevitable. Don Luis would not object, nor would his young bride, he would make sure of that.

"Tell me of your home in Cornwall, Sir Thomas." His silence frightened Maria Elena. She tried to walk on, but he had a hand firmly on her arm and in desperation she tried to find an interesting topic of conversation. "My father tells me it is a lovely spot. Will I be able to ride?"

"You'll find your time too occupied for such trivialities," Thomas murmured, moving closer to her. "At least for a while."

Maria Elena understood perfectly. Disgusted, she tried to free herself, but he was stronger than she anticipated and the next moment she found herself crushed against his huge chest. The smell of whisky was so strong that she felt sick, and then his mouth came down on hers, rough and clumsy. Despite his numerous women, Wyndham had never learned the finer arts of love-making. He took women to satisfy his own depraved nature and paid them handsomely afterwards. It never occurred to him to treat Maria Elena differently.

She almost fainted as she felt warm fingers trying to force their way down into the front of her bodice. All the restrained anger and disappointment broke loose inside her and gave her unexpected strength. Thomas reeled back under the stinging slaps she rained on his face and stood staring at her. Then to her dismay he began to chuckle, his fingers roving over the red marks already beginning to show on his cheeks.

"I prefer a woman with spirit," he said unpleasantly. "I'll enjoy instructing you in my ways, and now is as good a time as any to begin."

He reached for her again, but Maria Elena avoided his grasping hands and picking up her skirts, she fled along the narrow path.

"Come back, you little fool."

She did not heed the angry voice behind her, in fact the sound of his voice gave wings to her feet. Breathless she halted by a huge clump of bushes and heard him lumbering close behind her. She turned to run only to discover she had come to the end of the path. To one side of her was a high wall and on the other, a thickly wooded area, black and menacing.

A tall shape loomed up out of the trees. It was not Thomas, he was behind her, then who . . .? A shaft of moonlight fell across a scarred cheek and she stepped back, a hand against her throat. The scream which rose to her throat never materialised. A rough hand covered her mouth, an arm encircled her waist, pinioning her arms to her sides, and she was lifted bodily from the ground and borne into the inky blackness of the trees.

She was held too tightly to struggle, and the hand across her mouth silenced her cry of alarm. She had escaped from one man she loathed only to fall into the hands of another, far more dangerous. What did he mean to do, kill her?

"I mean you no harm," Adam MacDonald whispered in excellent Castilian. "Keep quiet and he'll give up looking for you in a while. Friend Thomas was not endowed with the virtue of patience."

Without knowing why, Maria Elena obeyed him and as she relaxed in his hold, so the tight band around her waist also relaxed. Thomas Wyndham had reached the end of the path. He stood looking about him and cursing profusely, but when there was no answer to his demands that Maria Elena show herself, he shrugged and returned the way he had come.

"No doubt he'll find a serving wench to console his hurt pride," Adam murmured, this time in English, and removed his hand from her mouth.

Maria Elena twisted her head to look up at the sharp profile above her. Without warning his mouth was on hers, in a kiss so wild and passionate it robbed her of all speech for some considerable time after he had released her. It demanded everything, yet gave nothing in return.

"A small price to pay for saving your honour," he mocked.

"Are you suggesting Sir Thomas would – would have—" Maria Elena broke off in disgust. "He would not dare." Pride forbade her to confess he had guessed the truth.

"You're obviously immune to his faults. He's a whoremonger. He's tumbled more women than you have hairs on your head," Adam retorted, and his voice rang with contempt.

Maria Elena raised her hand to strike his grinning features, but he fixed her with a stern look and said.

"If you're thinking of repaying me as you did Wyndham, forget it, it would be a bad mistake. The second you've made."

"Oh, what was the first?"

At last Maria Elena found her voice again. How glad she was of the darkness which hid her burning cheeks.

"That was in coming to England at all."

"You are insulting, sir. Release me at once, I wish to return to my apartments. If you do not, I shall call for a guard and have you whipped for daring to lay hands on the daughter of a grandee of Spain."

Maria Elena's hands pushed down on the arm which still encircled her waist. For a moment she thought he intended to refuse, then it slackened and fell away. Instead he gripped her by the wrist and led her back to the path, where he let her go and stood, hands on hips, regarding her with a smile as she smoothed down the skirts of her gown. Maria Elena's fear of him still remained, although she had recovered most of her composure. She was annoyed and dismayed he had seen her undignified struggle with Thomas Wyndham, and even had the effrontery to comment on it.

"Please allow me to pass."

"I'll see you safely to your apartments."

"There is no need, Captain MacDonald. I shall feel safer alone."

"Don't be afraid, you're safe in my company for the moment. You're under the Queen's protection and I'll not incur her displeasure, but once you leave London, that is a different matter."

Her brother had called him a murdering pirate and Maria Elena had been unable to believe that anyone could be so cruel as the man he described, but now as she stared into Adam's smiling face she saw the eyes were hard and merciless and she believed. She was suddenly glad she was spending only one night in the palace. Tomorrow she would be on her way to Cornwall, and a new life into which he could not intrude.

"What kind of man are you?" she breathed.

"One who hates the house of Choulqueras so savagely, nothing is going to stand in the way of my determination to destroy it."

"What has my brother ever done to you, or my father?" she demanded.

Adam's eyes narrowed to angry slits. Not for a moment did he believe she knew nothing of the crimes of her family.

"It'll give me great pleasure to relate them to you in detail one day."

"And me, Captain MacDonald, am I to be killed too?"

The corners of the lean mouth tightened.

"I think you'll be more useful to me alive."

Maria Elena caught her breath. She did not want to think what was implied by those words.

"I will find my own way back," she said stiffly and moved past him, her head held high, somehow containing the anguished tears until she reached the sanctuary of her room.

It took Ninetta three hours to undress her mistress and prepare her for bed and she was so distressed that the little maid curled up in a chair beside the bed and remained there all night.

Lady Caroline Stacey was not in her apartments. The gawky girl of seventeen who served as her maid grinned knowingly when Adam said he would call again later that evening, and almost earned herself a boxed ear.

Adam found himself yearning for the company of old friends as he left the palace. He returned to the house only long enough to change into more suitable attire and then he rode through the streets, already heavy with mist, to the small hamlet of Wapping.

The tavern called Hades overlooked the river and had been a favourite haunt since the days he sailed with his father. The men who frequented it were sailors like himself and despite the fact most of them were loud-mouthed drunkards when on shore, he preferred their company to any he found elsewhere, save for that of Francis Drake. They supped often at the tavern and watched the cock-fights in the cellars which ran out beneath the river.

The atmosphere was rowdy; drink and women were plentiful for hungry men fresh from the seas with their pockets full of money and fights were a regular occurrence. It was not unknown for some luckless sailor, drunk and penniless, to find himself a victim of the press gangs which roved the waterfront recruiting for the Navy.

Adam bought a tankard of strong Malmsey ale and pushed his way through the crowded tap room to the Aft Cabin and out on to the lower balcony which hung over the river. At high tide it was necessary to batten up the doorway to prevent the water seeping into the rooms beyond. The river was quiet tonight and heavy with mist as always, but he was able to make out the long slim line of a brigantine and he smiled in the darkness. His first mate had done well. It was a good feeling to have the *Nemesis* near at hand.

"Capitan, come and join us."

The dim light from the Aft Cabin framed a slight figure in the doorway behind Adam.

"Paco, I didn't see you when I came in."

"The boys are below in the pit. The first mate, he is very drunk, wants to fight everybody."

Adam grimaced and quickly finished his drink.

"This could turn out to be an expensive evening," he said dryly.

Adam's hatred of the Spanish race had one exception, the young pickpocket who had helped him escape from a Spanish jail five years before. At sea he was Adam's shadow and had been instrumental in averting death from his *compadre* on more than one occasion. He was barely five feet tall and the *Nemesis* crew had baited him mercilessly until Adam had instructed him in the use of a knife – now no man argued with him, and he had become indispensable.

Abel Black's raucous tones could be heard well above everyone else's as Adam descended the stairs. The cellar was full of men and women, supposedly there to watch the cockfights in the small arena in the centre of the floor. A few men were clustered around it feverishly betting, others were making merry with the whores and servant girls thoughtfully provided by the tavern to care for lonely seamen, but the majority of people were gathered about Abel Black, swearing, laughing, eager for a fight.

"He is very drunk, no?" Paco asked, with a grin.

"Very drunk, yes," Adam returned amusedly.

"The Duchess is not happy. She say we have to leave."

"Who's she?"

"The new owner. The Señor Luke is no longer here."

Paco vaulted on to a table and stared over the heads of the crowd and then pointed out a heavily painted woman moving in their direction.

Petticoats in charge of a tavern, Adam thought disgustedly. If she wasn't careful, she wouldn't have a place to run.

"Are you in charge of these scum?"

She stopped a few feet away from him, her face half hidden in the shadow; a jewelled hand lifting the skirts of her dress to avoid a man sprawled on the ground before her.

"Your choice of words doesn't apply to my men, madam," Adam growled. Delving into his doublet he pulled out a bag of gold and tossed it on to the floor at her feet. "That will cover any damage they do."

He had a brief glimpse of flaxen hair and a thickly powdered face as the woman bent to pick up the money. She weighed it in one hand.

"Your first mate will do more wrecking than this'll cover."

"Then send someone to my house tomorrow to collect the remainder. Ask anyone where Adam MacDonald lives, I'm well-known. You would be better engaged in pleasing your customers instead of bleeding them dry, or you may not have any."

He turned on his heel and started back up the stairs two at a time. Paco caught up with him at the door.

"*Capitano*, wait. She said you are to find a table and she will send a girl to you – one who won't pick your pocket. If she does I will slit her throat," Paco added with a grin.

"Convey my regrets to the Duchess and tell her I have a prior engagement," Adam answered sarcastically.

"And the girl, *capitano*?"

"She's yours."

The Duchess came into the tap room in time to see Adam disappearing through the outer door. Paco delivered his message and left her to go and seek his companion for the evening.

After a moment or two, the woman walked across the room, disdainfully ignoring the invitations from the men on both sides to sit and drink with them. She was well known for her fastidious choice of company and most of the invitations were to amuse her.

"I'm going to my room," she said to the burly man behind the bar. "Don't disturb me again tonight."

Upstairs the sound of laughter and shouting was still clear as she closed the door of the bedroom behind her. She lighted the lamp on the dressing table and sat down. The face staring back at her through the mirror was heavy with powder and rouge, and under the strong light beside her the small pox-scars were more noticeable. Slowly she began to remove the rings from her fingers, the heavy necklace from her throat, dropping them on to the dressing table one by one, a crooked smile on her lips. To her surprise she found that her hands were trembling and it took a large glass of rum to steady them sufficiently to unfasten her gown.

Her first sight of him in ten years and he had not recognised her. He thought he had been talking to a whore, and she had seen the contempt in his eyes and inwardly winced. Surely she could not care after so long?

"If you do you're a bloody fool," Sarah MacDonald said to the disfigured reflection.

CHAPTER THREE

THE house in St. James's was all in darkness as Adam let himself in. Somewhere in the distance the watch was calling twelve o'clock. Caroline would be waiting for him after the Queen had retired. It would take no time at all to change and go back to the palace.

He was about to open the door of his room when a faint sound from inside froze his hand on the door-handle. Instantly Adam thought of Don Luis. Only he, or Manuel, would dare invade the privacy of his home. On second thoughts it was probably a hired assassin, the Don was too important to do his own dirty work. With a tight smile Adam reached into his sleeve and drawing out his dirk flung wide the doors.

A ripple of amused laughter came from the direction of the four-poster bed as he slipped stealthily into the room.

"What the devil . . .?"

Stretched out on his bed was Caroline Stacey. She wore one of his robes loosely belted around her waist and it was obvious from the way it clung to her figure that she wore nothing beneath. Quietly closing the doors behind him, he crossed the room and looked down at her, restraining the urge to reach out and possess her full, red mouth.

"How did you get in?"

Caroline smoothed back the long red hair flowing past her shoulders like tongues of fire.

"I told your manservant you were expecting me. By the way you came in, perhaps you were hoping someone else would be here."

"You're lucky I wasn't feeling nervous," Adam said dryly, and sheathed his weapon.

Caroline's lips pursed in annoyance as he left her side to pour himself a glass of whisky from the bottle Jamie had thoughtfully left on the table. He was always casual with her, sometimes to such an infuriating extent she flew into a temper and threatened never to let him touch her again. But she always did. She was the kind of woman who enjoyed being dominated and it was a relief when Adam returned to England and she could enjoy the company of a real man instead of the fawning youths and dandies she used to amuse her while he was away.

"I was afraid you might not come to me tonight," she said softly. "Where have you been?"

"Nowhere that concerns you."

Adam swallowed his drink, watching her body grow taut beneath the robe as she stretched languidly.

"How long have you been at sea, Adam?"

"Five months."

She laughed and extended a hand towards him.

"An eternity for a man like you. Why are you waiting? Come here."

Adam crossed to the bed and caught her hand and pulled her unceremoniously from the bed. She slid on to the floor with a startled cry and lay there looking up at him with smouldering eyes, ignoring the half-open robe revealing her naked thighs.

Relaxing down on to the silken covers Adam said quietly. "Now, you come here."

Caroline twisted around in the arms encircling her and stared into the bronzed face a few inches away.

"How long are you staying this time?"

"Weeks, perhaps months, it depends."

"On Don Luis?"

Adam opened his eyes and looked at her and they were cold with suspicion.

"Why should it depend on the Spaniard?"

"I – I don't know," Caroline stammered, "but you must admit it was a little out of character for you to play Sir Galahad to Don Luis' daughter."

News travelled fast, Adam thought. Some scullery maid and her lover had probably been in the garden at the same time.

"She's very attractive."

"So that's it! She's taken your fancy. You'll have a hard time tumbling that one with her brother around. Is that your intention?"

"I've never cold-bloodedly seduced a woman in my life. The thought never entered my head, but by God it might be amusing to melt that little icicle," Adam chuckled.

He ducked as Caroline's nails raked at his cheeks and leant up, pinning her beneath him. She called him an obscene name because he refused to stop laughing and then his mouth was on hers and as her arms locked about his neck, all thought of the other woman vanished from her mind.

When Adam awoke again, it was morning and Caroline was already preparing to leave. She had been his mistress for over two years and neither had any complaints. He fulfilled her demands to be dominated and she satisfied his need for a woman. Their association was uncluttered by worthless sentiment. Perhaps that was why he had stayed with her for so long, Adam mused as he watched her.

"Come and dine with me tonight," he said.

"If I can. I may not be free until very late. The Queen is entertaining Don Luis Choulqueras tonight, which means she will be in a foul temper all day. She loathes his company and takes it out on us." She smiled at the sudden interest in Adam's eyes. "No, she won't be there. She is leaving for Sir Thomas' estates in Cornwall this morning."

"My interest in her isn't what you believe."

"I know you, Adam, a pretty face is a challenge."

"Not this one. Does she travel alone?" Adam climbed out of bed and began to dress thoughtfully.

"No, with her brother and a retinue of the Queen's guard. Sir Thomas was to go too, but Don Luis has postponed the wedding and so he must remain in London. I heard the Queen discussing it last night with Captain Drake; apparently the ship bringing the bride's dowry and the family priest who is to perform the ceremony, is now not due to arrive until next week and without them there can be no marriage."

If he had his way the ship would never arrive, Adam thought as he escorted Caroline downstairs and made arrangements for her to be driven back to the palace. With the *Nemesis* near at hand he would be able to slip away unobtrusively and return the same way. He found himself wondering if the charms of Maria Elena Choulqueras would be enough to hold Thomas Wyndham when he learned she brought him no dowry.

For almost a week Adam played the idle man about court. He wined and dined Caroline at his house or in one of the more respectable taverns along the river. He appeared at the gambling tables often and rode every morning through the Manor of the Hyde, as was the custom of most young gentlemen of that day. To any watching eyes, and he was sure there were many, his behaviour was impeccable.

While Adam kicked his heels and patiently waited, others were more busily occupied.

With the Babington conspirators safely dead and Mary cooped up in Fotheringay Castle, her health ruined, reputation blackened by distorted facts and misinterpreted actions and deserted by her only son, the time was ripe for the trap to close on the unfortunate Queen of Scots.

The second week in October brought an assorted group of people to the castle. Judges, peers and Privy Councillors, among them the Lord Treasurer Burleigh, Sir Amyas Paulet, the Earls of Oxford, Worcester, Cumberland and many others. These were members of the court commissioned to try Mary Stuart. They brought with them a letter from the Queen of England.

The cruel bluntness of the wording took away Mary's breath, but she remained composed, refusing to betray increasing fears for her safety. Elizabeth made no bones about the fact that she believed her cousin to have been the leader of the plots against her life. Her only hope was to confess all to the commission and throw herself on their mercy.

Mary raised her eyes from the letter and stared at the impassive faces before her. Sir Amyas Paulet looked away, unable to bear the tortured look on the face of the woman he had secretly come to respect. And then an odd smile flitted across her face as she slowly tore the parchment into pieces and allowed the fragments to trickle through her fingers on to the stone floor. Elizabeth had her answer. It was the beginning of the end.

"You are very quiet, sister."

Manuel Choulqueras dismissed the servant hovering at his elbow and looked across the dinner table at Maria Elena's pale features. The sea air had not improved her health, she looked terrible. When she did not reply his face darkened angrily.

"In the name of heaven, are you deaf as well as dumb?"

Maria Elena pushed away the plate of food in front of her, untouched and laid down her napkin. At length she looked up at her brother.

"Have we anything to say to each other, Manuel?"

They had been at Sir Thomas' estates for five days and they were the longest, dreariest days she had ever known. It was a gaunt, palatial house high on the cliffs and so close to the sea, she had found it impossible to sleep for the first two nights because of the waves crashing inshore below her window. Everywhere she went she was aware of the growing need for repairs and redecoration. She knew that her future husband was no pauper, yet it seemed he preferred to spend his money on gambling and women instead of on his family home. Nothing could be kept secret for long at court and Maria Elena had been fully acquainted with all his faults before she left.

It had been almost a relief to reach Cornwall, at least until she saw where she was to live. The rooms were damp and cold and her duennas had both gone down with colds and were confined to their beds. Apart from her faithful Ninetta and her brother, Maria Elena had no one to talk to. Rather than sit in the company of the latter and come under the lash of his scornful tongue, she remained closeted in her room, growing to feel more like a prisoner as the days passed.

"Father Paulus should arrive soon and your trousseau, but even the magnificence of your wedding gown will do little to improve your appearance." Manuel leaned towards her frowning at the dark smudges beneath her eyes. It would not do to have her looking like this on her wedding day. "You look tired, my dear, have an early night. Instruct Ninetta you are to stay in bed until midday tomorrow and then we will ride together. The scenery is primitive, but not unattractive. Would you like that?"

"Yes, Manuel, I would." There was no answering smile on his sister's face. He wanted to be sure Thomas Wyndham was pleased with his bargain and he did not care a fig how she really felt. The loneliness of her position made her heart ache. "Perhaps an early night is all I need to dispel this awful tiredness. Goodnight, Manuel."

"Goodnight. I will not disturb you."

"Thank you."

Maria Elena was too surprised to say more and quickly hurried upstairs. Manuel was indeed worried not to demand to hear her at her prayers.

Ninetta rose from the chair beside the fire.

"Are you going to bed so soon, my lady?"

"Yes, I am very tired."

Maria Elena sat down on the tapestry-covered stool before the dressing-table and the maid began to brush her hair. Ninetta was worried too, but she would not presume to confide her thoughts, even though her mistress hardly ever spoke crossly to her and had never struck her. Not like the other servants in the Choulqueras household, who were subjected to blows and violent outbursts of temper especially from the unpredictable Manuel. She was also afraid that their conversation might be overheard by one of the servants of her future master and bring about her dismissal. She liked Thomas Wyndham even less than did Maria Elena.

She lingered in the room after Maria Elena was in bed. She stood by the window looking out over the sea and listening to the lusty howl of the wind. Although there was no moon, it seemed unusually light. From the direction of the village came a curious red glow, lighting up the sky for some considerable distance.

"Go to bed, Ninetta," her mistress murmured sleepily.

The girl turned, about to mention the strange light, then she shrugged her shoulders. It was probably only a haystack on fire.

"Goodnight, my lady. May the blessed saints watch over you and give you a good rest."

But no one in the house on the cliffs was to sleep peacefully that night, any more than the unfortunate people in the small village a mile away where homes were already ablaze, husbands and sons being savagely cut down while women and children were carried screaming to the black-sailed ships anchored off the point.

Maria Elena was dreaming of the gardens at St. James's and her unpleasant encounter with Thomas. Again his hands were reaching out for her, his face coming closer to hers. She awoke to find it was no dream but horrifying reality. There were men in the room, huge, bearded, dark-skinned men with golden earrings and curved gleaming swords in their hands. Most of them were naked from the waist upwards. In the doorway Ninetta was struggling in the grip of one of them and cursing profusely in Spanish. From below came screams of pain intermingled with laughter and the air was thick with smoke.

Maria Elena was pulled bodily from the bed. As rough hands bruised her bare shoulders, she began to kick and rake at the cheeks of her captor with her long nails, but she made no impression on the huge Negro. Her last recollection was of being thrown over his shoulder as if she was a sack of grain, before she faded into merciful oblivion.

The Barbary pirates made a good haul that night. Their ships slipped away as silently as they came. Behind they left a burning village and numerous dead and injured, and a blazing inferno high on the cliff top. Thomas Wyndham no longer had a house for his bride – he no longer had a bride.

Chained in pitiful conditions in the holds of the slave ships were thirty assorted women and children, among them Maria Elena and Ninetta and Manuel, whose life had been saved by the richness of his clothing. Prisoners such as these would fetch high prices in the slave markets of the Barbary coast.

News of the raid, not an unusual occurrence along that part of the English coast, reached London in the form of a sixteen-year-old boy who had miraculously escaped the fate meted out to his father and two brothers. Within an hour of the boy being carried exhausted into Elizabeth's presence, Francis Drake had been roused from the warmth of his bed, given explicit instructions and speeded on his way to Tilbury.

Sending orders on ahead by a special messenger, he made a detour to Adam MacDonald's house and was admitted, not by a servant, but by Adam himself. Drake noted he was fully dressed and sighed gratefully.

"Thank God – you've heard. How soon can you sail?"

A tiny frown puckered Adam's brows.

"Within the hour. Why?"

"To go after the Corsairs, why else are you dressed at this hour?"

"My plans have been made for the last three days. You and I are talking at cross purposes. What am I supposed to know," Adam demanded quietly.

"Barbary pirates raided the Cornish coast late last night. They burned and pillaged with their usual exuberance. God knows how many poor souls they took with them." Drake paused to let his words sink in. "They captured Manuel Choulqueras and his sister. The Queen has ordered me to go after them and not to return until I have them safe on board the *Revenge*."

"That means going into dangerous waters, my friend."

Adam's expression betrayed no emotion. His appointment with the treasure ship was unimportant compared with this unexpected opportunity.

"Not necessarily. The *Nemesis* is anchored at Wapping. You can be at sea at least six hours before me," Francis Drake said. "Go after them, Adam. The Queen has sanctioned her approval for all privateers to put to sea."

"I think your determination to recover the girl safely is fogging your brain," Adam replied coldly. "I'll not lift a finger to help any member of the Choulqueras family, and I suggest you don't ask me to do so again."

He picked up his cloak and fastened it around his shoulders, unwavering before his friend's disbelieving gaze.

"You can't mean that. You know better than I what will happen not only to her, but all the women."

"If you're trying to appeal to my better nature, Francis, forget it, I don't have one. It gives me great pleasure to think of the suffering the girl and her brother will have to endure."

Francis Drake spun around on his heel and disappeared through the front door before Adam had finished speaking. Adam made no attempt to follow him and began to pull on his thick riding gloves thoughtfully. His ship was faster than the slave ships which were heavy with booty. It was a heaven-sent opportunity he could not refuse.

"Who was that?"

He glanced up at the staircase to where Caroline stood, clutching a flimsy chemise about her. He had forgotten he had left her sleeping in his bed.

"Weren't you listening?"

"Of course I was." She leaned over the balustrade, smiling down at him. "Can't you stay a while longer?"

"No, I must sail with the tide if I am to catch our pirate friends."

Caroline started and drew back, her eyes accusing.

"You liar, you are going after her."

"The carriage will take you back to the palace at seven," Adam mocked. "I'll see you when I get back."

He left her standing at the top of the staircase, her beautiful face contorted with fury. He had been longing after the Spanish girl while he was making love to her. Caroline had visions of him slipping away from her. If she did not have him, she would make sure no other woman did, certainly not Maria Elena Choulqueras. She hurried back to the bedroom, her lips pressed tightly together. It would be interesting to find out how much Don Luis would pay for the information she had to offer.

Maria Elena sat with her back against the wooden bulwark, listening to the pitiful sound of sobbing from the women somewhere in the darkness beside her. She wanted to cry too, but the tears would not come, despite the agonising pain in her arms. Her wrists were shackled together above her head with the heavy chains connected to a stout ring in the wooden beams. Beside her, Manuel and several others had been treated the same way, while the rest of the prisoners were chained by the ankles. A few of the women had been spared the cruel chains, only to be subjected to far worse indignities. They were made to feed their companions and carry food for the crew, and at night they were taken out of the hold to amuse the pirates. Ninetta was one of these.

Maria Elena had prayed for their deliverance and thanked God the pirates considered her to be too important a piece of merchandise to treat her in this fashion. She had lost count of time. It was impossible to tell how long ago she had been dragged from her bed and confined in the evil-smelling, rat-infested hold. It might have been hours – or days.

"Manuel," she turned wide, frightened eyes in the direction of her brother. "Are we to be sold as slaves?"

"Of course not, *stupido*, we are far too important. They will demand a ransom for us."

"But how do they know who we are?"

"Because I told them. Why else do you think they didn't kill me?" Her brother snapped coldly.

Maria Elena did not reply. When she had recovered consciousness to find Manuel beside her, she thought he had been captured trying to help her; now she knew that his presence on board when no other male prisoners had been taken, was proof that he had blurted out his identity in order to save his own life. The realisation that he was a coward did not greatly surprise her, it only deepened her despair. Wordlessly she turned away from him and pretended to sleep.

The pirates rarely bothered to inspect the prisoners. They had captured more than enough to make the journey worthwhile. The price the new slaves would fetch in the markets, coupled with the ransom for the two Spaniards, would make it a rich haul, it mattered none if one or two died en route.

Maria Elena heard the shouting on deck, but took little notice until there came the sound of cannons and the ship suddenly shuddered as if it had been hit. Immediately there were screams and wails of terror from the women about her. She drew herself back as far as possible against the side of the hold and closed her eyes, silently praying.

As time progressed it became obvious to everyone the pirate vessel was under attack.

"Perhaps it is one of our ships," Maria Elena suggested hopefully. "Oh, Manuel, are we to be saved—" Her voice trailed off as the hatches were flung open and sunlight streamed into the gloom, momentarily blinding all below.

Amid the crying of the children and the sobbing of women, a voice shouted in English.

"For God's sake show a light down here."

Several figures swung themselves down into the hold and burning torches were handed down to them.

"Enough of this cat o' wailing," Abel Black growled. "We're here to help ye." He moved slowly in a circle, holding the torch high to see the faces of those about him. He halted before Maria Elena and her brother and both saw his eyes light up. "Paco, fetch the Capt'n, they're here."

"I am Manuel Mendoza de Choulqueras, son of Luis—" Manuel did not finish the sentence and his jaw dropped visibly as Paco came slithering down to rejoin his companion and behind him, another man dropped nimbly into the hold. Torchlight flickered over a scarred cheek and glittering eyes and Maria Elena gave a little scream. It was impossible not to recognise that arrogant face. Beside her mistress, Ninetta crossed herself and began to pray.

"Free the prisoners and put them aboard the *Nemesis*," Adam MacDonald ordered. "See to it they have everything they need and be sure they are not molested. They have suffered enough."

"And these three?" Paco asked, motioning to Manuel and Ninetta, who had her arms protectively around Maria Elena. "Shall I slit their throats? All except the one with big eyes, eh – this one I like." He beamed at Ninetta and was answered by a frightened squeal.

"Help Abel get the women out of here before the ship goes down and takes us with it," Adam retorted. "You can come back to the girl later."

He spoke without diverting any attention from Maria Elena's stricken face. The conditions he found her in appalled him, although he had seen worse on Spanish slave ships and prisoners who had received far harsher treatment. The pirates had obviously intended a better fate for her, than for her companions.

"What do you intend to do with us, MacDonald?"

Adam did not miss the quaver of fear in Manuel's voice and his eyes gleamed. Maria Elena heard it too and saw the reaction, and her heart failed her. They were still prisoners, this time without the chance of ransom. She felt certain they were to be killed.

"You will enjoy the hospitality of the *Nemesis* for a while," came the calm reply, "although I find it tempting to leave you here as food for the fishes."

"Then you mean us no harm." Manuel brightened, his hopes rising. Of course they were safe, they were still under the Queen of England's protection. "You were sent to rescue us."

"I came of my own accord – to settle old scores," Adam answered. "Paco, loose the woman's chains and take her to my cabin. The maid can go with her. As for the other one, chain him in the hold with the rest of the rats."

"Captain MacDonald."

"Yes, señorita?"

Maria Elena did not waver before his penetrating gaze, although she was trembling inwardly.

"Is it your intention to kill us? If so, I beg of you to leave us here. Drowning does not appeal to me, but I somehow think I shall prefer it to the end you plan for us."

It took the last of Maria Elena's courage to keep her voice steady and Adam felt begrudging admiration stir within him. She was only a slip of a girl, yet she possessed more courage in her frail body than the excuse for a man beside her. He knew Manuel to be a coward; bullies nearly always were.

He looked into the face of the Spaniard – into the face of

fear – and then into that of the girl beside him, so contrastingly calm. Without answering he turned and motioned two of his crew to come below.

"Take them aboard the *Nemesis*," he ordered, and returned on deck.

The pirate vessel was sinking rapidly. The water was already seeping into the lower part of the hold as Manuel and Maria Elena were brought up. After the long confinement in the dark she could hardly see, and her legs refused to give her support. It was Adam who lifted her and she felt the enormous strength of this man as he swung her over the side into the arms of a waiting sailor. She saw her brother being hustled roughly away and called out to him, but if he heard he neither answered nor looked round. She was carried below and through a well-furnished cabin into a smaller one beyond where she was thrown down on to the bed. Ninetta came running through the door to fling herself beside her mistress.

"My lady, don't cry." She stared in dismay at the tears welling down over Maria Elena's cheeks. "He must not see you like this."

"I cannot help it. I am so afraid. Is my brother safe?"

"*Si*, they have put him in one of the holds. I heard the captain order him to be fed on biscuits and water for the journey."

"That man is a devil, Ninetta, he intends to kill us, I am sure."

The sound of shouting drew Ninetta to the window.

"The ship is sinking," she gasped and crossed herself. "There are men still on the decks. Holy Mother of Mercy, it is gone; oh, those poor devils!"

"Do not weep for them, *niña*, they would have sold you into slavery. They are not worthy of your pity," Paco said from the doorway.

Maria Elena started up in alarm, expecting to see Adam MacDonald's tall frame behind him, but the boy was alone and she sank back on to the bed in relief. Paco laid down the tray he was carrying. It held a bowl of water and bandages. He looked down at Maria Elena and felt no pity for her, despite the fact that they were both Spanish. She was nobility and Paco Romerez had suffered greatly at the hands of such people. Had it not been for his compadre Adam, he would have suffered hanging long ago, just because he had smiled at the daughter of one of the richest men in his village. He had also picked her father's pocket at the same time.

"The captain wishes you to be comfortable. Food will be brought to you in a short while. The water is to bathe the marks on your wrists."

Maria Elena stared down at the two red circles of raw skin where the heavy chains had continually chafed. She was both surprised and grateful that her captor had noticed, for they were exceedingly painful, yet she could find no words of thanks – not for Adam MacDonald.

"Be gone then, and let me tend my mistress," Ninetta ordered shrilly.

The first time this handsome boy had come near her she had become aware of something she should not feel. He was a pirate too, and a traitor to his own people. She had no doubt he would be like all the rest and as always she would learn to submit. She was a servant, a nobody. Her parents had been peasants of the lowest class who had sold her into service in return for enough money to feed the newest baby.

Ninetta had been ten years old. By the time she was fifteen she had learned it was easier to submit to the demands of her various masters, than endure a whipping. She had borne manhandling from old men who engaged a pretty girl for duties other than those of a normal servant and from the inexperienced sons of the house, eager to try out their manhood on someone unable to refuse.

It had been this way until she came into the Choulqueras household at the age of seventeen, bitter and disillusioned with her life, but by now completely resigned to it. Maria Elena was unlike any mistress she had ever served. She was gentle and understanding and unusually generous. Soon Ninetta became her personal maid and found herself accepted as a friend instead of a servant, much to the jealousy of the duennas who had fiercely guarded her since birth and considered her their property.

It was about this time that Ninetta had come under the interested eye of Manuel Choulqueras. She knew of his reputation with the female servants in the house and prayed he would never become taken with her, but the inevitable happened. Returning to the house late at night after an absence of several months, he had had Ninetta deliberately roused from her bed in order to show him to his apartments. She did not return to the servants' quarters and that night she had discovered that everything she had been told about him was true. As a lover he was cruel and unbelievably cold. Ninetta had not attracted him because she was pretty, but because she was part of the household, a possession, a chattel, and that was exactly how Manuel treated her on that and every other occasion he demanded her presence.

She thought of confessing everything to Maria Elena, but was warned against this in such a manner that she grew afraid for her life. For months she went in terror of becoming pregnant, but as time passed and no child came, Manuel's interest in her faded and he had not touched her for almost a year. They had been the happiest months Ninetta had known.

And now there was this young Spaniard who looked at her with a smile on his face and an invitation in his eyes. Yes, he would be like all the others, she thought sadly.

It was evening. Ninetta sat on the window seat, her head resting in her arms. Stretched out on the bed, Maria Elena lay in a feverish half-sleep. Paco had brought them food and there was sweet wine to wash down a surprisingly tasty meal. Neither of the women had realised how hungry they were until the full dishes were uncovered. No one came near them and there seemed to be great activity on deck. They heard voices sometimes from the outer cabin and as darkness fell, the sound of revelry above increased. At least someone had something to celebrate, Maria Elena thought bitterly.

A shaft of light suddenly filled the cabin and a shadow fell across her.

"You are resting, good," Adam said. "Five days in chains will sap the strength of the strongest man, let alone a woman."

Maria Elena blinked up at him unbelievingly.

"Was it as long as that?" she whispered.

"I'm not surprised you lost count of time. Still, it's over now. The journey home will seem nothing, I promise you."

"Home? Are you taking us back to England?"

A crooked smile tugged at the corners of his mouth.

"Where else?"

He looked around at Ninetta, now sitting bolt upright, her eyes fixed on Paco who was lounging in the doorway.

"Go with Paco, he'll find somewhere for you to sleep," he ordered.

"She can stay with me," Maria Elena protested. "I ask nothing for myself because I know the hate you bear me, but do not subject her to any more brutality, she has suffered enough."

"Do not plead for me, my lady, I will go with him."

Ninetta rose to her feet and came to Adam's side, her face pale and tense.

"If you lay hands on my mistress, I will kill you," she said vehemently.

"You have a spitfire there, Paco, are you sure you still want her?" Adam murmured.

Paco smiled and nodded. Taking the maid's arm, he led her out of the cabin and closed the door behind them.

"Have you no pity, how can you let him take her?" Maria Elena asked appalled.

"He won't harm her, believe me."

"You ask the impossible, Captain MacDonald."

"You are obviously feeling better," Adam said humourlessly.

Despite his hatred of her family, he recognised that she had undergone a terrifying experience and was near to breaking point. It did not show in her defiant expression, but in the slim hands clenching and unclenching at her sides. He moved closer to the bed, holding out the glass of brandy he had brought with him.

"Drink this, it'll help."

Maria Elena stared at it in silence, then in a voice that trembled she said, "You have made it clear by bringing me to your cabin you intend to dishonour me. I will not make it easier for you by drinking that."

To her dismay he threw back his head and roared with laughter.

"What a child you are! If rape was in my mind, I wouldn't need to ply you with unlimited quantities of liquor first. Now – or later, you would give me little trouble. I thought this might help you to sleep after your ordeal. Drink it – or leave it, it makes no difference to me."

He put down the glass on the table beside the bed and opened the door. Then he turned slowly and his expression was no longer amused. He stared at her with such intense scrutiny Maria Elena instinctively drew back, acutely conscious how the remains of her nightgown scarcely covered half of her body. Her thighs showed through large rents in the side, it was torn from the shoulders, exposing more of her than decency allowed. Beneath his gaze she felt completely unclothed.

"You have a high opinion of yourself, Maria Elena Choulqueras," he said flatly. "What makes you think you have anything I want?"

Maria Elena heard the key turn in the closed door as she sank back on to the bed, her cheeks flaming with colour. Exhausted, she slept.

Paco opened a door and ushered Ninetta inside a cabin filled full of crates and iron-bound chests.

"This is where the capitan keeps the fruits of our labours," he murmured. "Tonight you sleep with a fortune about you. It is good to be rich, no?"

Ninetta stared about her without answering. At length her eyes came to rest on the single bunk in one corner.

"Is that where I am to sleep?"

"*Si*."

She turned and looked at Paco, standing with his back against the door and a look of pain crossed her face. Slowly she began to unfasten her blouse, not daring to watch his eyes because she knew what she would see.

"Am I being invited to stay with you?" Paco asked quietly.

Ninetta's hands shook visibly. She finished removing her skirt before she looked up at him. He made no move to reach out and take her in his arms as she expected. His face was expressionless – unreadable. Beneath the thin white shift her body was pathetically thin and her arms were covered with bruises.

"Isn't that why I am here – to sleep with you? The others did not ask my permission, why should you?"

She began to tremble as he stepped towards her, his face softening.

"You have been ill-used, I can see that, and the other women told me things I did not like to hear. But why do you think I am the kind of man to take a woman by force?"

Ninetta stared at the finely chiselled features before her and saw compassion, not lust, in the liquid brown eyes. She was tired and confused at his lack of interest. wearily she shrugged her shoulders. She had become so used to force that she expected it from every man she met. Paco understood this and something more than pity flowed into his heart at the sight of this appealing little creature.

"Do you want me to stay with you?"

"Does it matter?"

"*Si*. Shall I go?"

"Yes, oh – no!" Ninetta's voice halted him as he reached the door. He wheeled about, the brown eyes smouldering and saw her face was wet with tears. "I don't know, I've never had a choice before."

Paco stepped forward, lifted her with great care and placed her on the low bunk. He covered her with the blankets there and leaned over her.

"You have one now."

"I think I want you to stay, but I am afraid. Yes, yes, I do."

"Then I will stay, my little one, but not tonight. You need to sleep and forget how you have been misused. Tonight it would give you no pleasure and therefore I would gain none also."

Ninetta caught her breath at his words. Was it possible there were men in the world who actually considered a woman's feelings in these matters?

"You are very kind—"

"I am also very patient," Paco murmured. "Goodnight, *mi niña*, sleep well for you are perfectly safe here. I will lock the door and keep the key around my neck all night."

His lips lightly brushed her damp cheek and then he was gone. Like her mistress Ninetta did not remain awake for long, but unlike Maria Elena whose sleep was plagued with nightmares, Ninetta slept blissfully, dreaming of Paco.

CHAPTER FOUR

A THUNDEROUS noise somewhere overhead rudely awoke Maria Elena next morning. Dazed with sleep, she lay listening to the sound of shouting and the heavy tread of feet on the deck above her head. It was several minutes before she became aware of her surroundings. The glass of brandy directly in her line of vision brought the incidents of the previous days flooding back into her mind.

Dragging herself out of bed, she ran to the window and saw another ship almost upon them. Its rigging was torn and there was a gaping hole in its side. It was the *Santa Margarita*, sister ship to the *San Cristobal*. Adam MacDonald was trying to steal her dowry. Whirling about, she flung herself against the door, screaming for someone to come and let her out, but of course no one came.

After the moment of hysteria had passed, she returned to the window to watch the crippled ship slowly being reduced to a shattered wreck by the smaller, faster *Nemesis*.

Suddenly the roar of cannons ceased from both vessels. The battle was almost done. The *Nemesis* keeled hard over, cutting through the water like a sleek, grey shark, and came alongside the enemy ship. Maria Elena saw men swarming up the rigging, some with grappling irons. Sunlight flashed on knives and swords as the furious fight broke out and the decks ran red with blood and were littered with the bodies of the dead and dying.

Sick and faint, Maria Elena fell to her knees beside the window seat, unable to watch any longer, and this was how Adam found her an hour later when the last of the

Spanish crew had been disposed of and the heavy chests from the hold of the *Santa Margarita*, brought on board. At first he thought she had been injured, but then he saw the window was still intact and there was no sign of debris in the cabin and he restrained the impulse to go forward and lift her up.

The eyes which rose to meet his were filled with loathing.

"You slaughtered them – like animals!"

"Which is what they were," Adam replied bleakly. "It was foolish of you to watch."

"For this outrage I shall make sure my father hangs you," Maria Elena snapped.

His dark eyes glittered with amusement. He stepped back, beckoning her to follow.

"I think there is someone you know in here."

"Father Paulûs! God has answered my prayers. I was afraid they had killed you too."

Maria Elena threw herself into the arms of the elderly man in priest's robes, who stood beside Abel Black and Paco.

"Hush, child, I am not hurt." The priest held her for a while, stroking the dishevelled hair and wondering at her appearance. Then he put her from him gently, his expression grave. "Have these men harmed you?"

Maria Elena blushed and lowered her eyes. Even if she had been seduced she would not have been able to confess it in front of grinning sailors, with Adam MacDonald lounging in a chair to one side of her, silent and menacing.

"Manuel and I were captured by Barbary pirates from the house of my future husband," she explained. "Captain MacDonald rescued us yesterday." The words almost stuck in her throat and she had to force them out. Later, when they were alone, she would tell him the truth.

"We are in your debt, Captain." Father Paulus turned to the young man in the chair. The girl was obviously afraid to speak in his presence. "I shall make it my business to acquaint Don Luis of your behaviour, no doubt he will wish to reward you himself."

"Of that I'm sure," Adam chuckled. "Paco, find a quiet place for the father to sleep. He is not to be molested."

"I want him to stay," Maria Elena protested.

"You'll have to wait a little longer to unburden your soul," Adam replied, rising to his feet. He stared down at his first mate, kneeling beside a chest piled high with gold ducats and silver ornaments of the most exquisite workmanship. Maria Elena gasped in horror as he kicked the lid shut and said smilingly. "Divide this between the men and throw in my share as a bonus for work well done."

"They'll be right glad o' the day they signed on with you, Capt'n" Abel Black grinned.

Adam closed the door behind his departing figure and turned to meet Maria Elena's angry gaze.

"I demand you bring back that chest."

"On board my own ship, no one questions my orders, señorita."

"But you know that was part of my dowry! It belongs to Sir Thomas."

"A pity he will never receive it," Adam said carelessly.

He began to inspect the two remaining chests, pulling out the carefully packed clothes and tossing them to one side as if they were mere rags.

"Take care! Oh, my beautiful dresses!" Maria Elena cried.

"I suggest you find yourself some clothes," Adam said, casting a sidelong glance at her nightgown.

He gave a soft exclamation and bent to pull out a dress of white brocade and lace, heavily encrusted with jewels. Maria Elena could stand it no longer.

"How dare you soil my wedding gown with bloodstained hands?" she cried angrily, and snatched it from his grasp.

Adam's eyes hardened as he stared at her standing in the

midst of the enormous wardrobe of priceless clothes. Her wedding gown in which she was to marry a Papist sympathiser, a man in the pay of Don Luis. Until that moment Adam had had no idea how she would be of use to him, but now he knew. There would be a wedding as planned, but with a different bridegroom, and when the Don learned his daughter was married to his enemy instead of the man he had personally chosen, honour would demand he challenged Adam to a duel. He nodded towards the dress she was hugging tightly against her breast.

"Put that on."

"I will not."

"For a wedding a bride must be suitably attired," he said softly. "Do not anger me, girl, or I'll send a couple of my men to prepare you."

"Prep – prepare me?" Maria Elena stammered. She stepped back from him, seized with a terrible fear, and the words he had spoken to her in the garden at St. James's came flooding back. "*You will be more useful to me alive.*"

"You can't mean to – to—" she broke off, her eyes dilating. "No, I won't marry you."

"The bride, the wedding gown and the priest – perhaps there is a God after all," Adam said as if she had not spoken.

"I would rather die than become the wife of a pirate, a thief and – and a murderer."

"Considering the high opinion you have of yourself, I'm surprised you were so willing to marry Wyndham. You are obviously not interested in the choice of husband, so long as he can satisfy your needs. You'll find me quite adequate – more of a man than that whoremonger."

Maria Elena blushed to the roots of her hair and drew back a hand to hit out at his sardonic features, but he averted the blow with a sharp downward movement of his hand that numbed every nerve in her arm.

"Don't be foolish enough to try that again,"

"Manuel will kill you!"

"No, I shall kill him. You could prolong his life if you are sensible."

"If I marry you he will live?"

"I make no bargains."

Adam watched her sink down into the huge leather covered chair behind his desk. She looked as if she might faint, but he made no move to help her. He was done with sentiment.

A knock on the cabin door diverted his attention. Paco came in.

"The priest is safely tucked away, *capitano*."

"It may be necessary to untuck him," Adam said with a humourless smile. Determinedly he turned back to Maria Elena. "Well?"

"Father Paulus knows I would never willingly agree to marry you. He will refuse to perform the ceremony."

"You'll become my wife of your own free will," Adam declared. He looked at Paco, whose mouth was gaping visibly. "Take the priest on deck and assemble the crew. Take your time about it and afterwards fetch the maid here. Then you are to go to the hold and wait. If the señorita is not on deck by the time I arrive, cut the Spaniard's throat and throw him overboard."

"*Si, Capitano*, with pleasure."

"You would not dare!"

Maria Elena sprang to her feet and stood swaying unsteadily, a hand against her wildly beating heart. The look on Adam's face told her he would carry out his threat.

"If – if I agree to this marriage, I will never let you lay your hands on me. I will kill myself first."

Adam threw her a glance which made it plain that if it pleased him, her unwillingness would not deter him.

"Do as you are told, Paco," he said quietly. "I will see you on deck, Señorita Choulqueras."

When Ninetta came into the cabin she found her mistress in the bedroom trying desperately to dress herself. It had never been necessary before, and Maria Elena was crying in vexation as she struggled to fasten her wedding gown.

"My lady, what are you doing?"

"Help me quickly," Maria Elena ordered. Her tone was sharper than she intended and she saw her maid flinch, but with her brother's life at stake, there was no time for explanations. "Have you gone deaf? Unless I am on deck before Captain MacDonald, Manuel is to be killed."

"Holy Mother of Jesus." Ninetta began to fasten the gown with trembling fingers. "What does he want with you?"

"I must marry him."

"You can't. What will Don Luis say?"

"Would you rather I allowed my brother to be murdered? My father will understand."

"But you have no idea what that terrible man has in store for you."

"Whatever Adam MacDonald wants, I am not in a position to refuse it."

Ninetta hurriedly brushed her mistress's hair and secured it back from her face with jewelled combs.

"Will he keep his word, once you are his wife?" she asked.

"For pity's sake, don't say such a thing, Ninetta or my courage will fail me. I have little enough to face him as it is. No, leave the veil." Maria Elena stared at herself in the mirror. Her eyes, red and swollen from continual crying, stood out against the chalk-white of her face. She bit her lips to bring some colour to them and declared wearily, "I will have to do."

"What about your jewels, my lady?"

Ninetta opened the small jewel-casket on the bed. It contained the most valuable of Maria Elena's jewellery, and had been hidden beneath a sumptuous array of silk nightgowns, and although Adam had found it, he had left it untouched.

Maria Elena gazed at the priceless gems arrayed on the dark velvet and a strange look entered her eyes.

"Why not?" She picked out a heavy emerald necklace mounted in gold and a matching ring. "There – at least now he will know he is not marrying a village woman," she said, and picking up her skirts, walked calmly out of the cabin.

As Ninetta closed the casket and prepared to follow, she realised Maria Elena had taken a poison ring.

On the upper deck on the *Nemesis* Father Paulus was ignoring the whispered sniggers from the crew gathered around him, and the jeering invitations to drink the health of their captain on his wedding day.

He was determined the ceremony would not take place. Maria Elena had obviously been forced in some way to agree. It was contrary to all laws of morality and the Church to marry her against her will. He would not have had the slightest hesitation had the bridegroom been Thomas Wyndham, but a common pirate, whose life expectancy was likely to be very short once Don Luis heard of his infamous conduct – it did not bear consideration.

A few yards away from him seated cross-legged on the hold cover, Paco was enthusiastically drinking wine from one of the flagon jars Adam had ordered to be distributed to the crew. Added to the extra booty, free, unlimited quantities of rich ale were the answer to heaven-sent prayers. Everyone from the first mate to the cabin boy was in a mood to celebrate.

A cheer went up as Adam came striding through their midst. His battle-stained clothes had been discarded and replaced with new black breeches and a white shirt with lace ruffles which made his sunburnt skin appear even darker. The long Spanish sword with its fine Toledo blade hung by his side. He glanced at his men and smiled good humouredly.

"When those jars are empty there are more in the store

room," he said and joined Father Paulus. "Is everything ready?"

"It is not. You may have forced that poor unfortunate girl below to agree to this farce, but I will not. It is unthinkable for a man with your background – your vile way of living – to presume to take as your wife a child whose family is one of the most revered in Cartagena. Such a marriage will never have the sanction or the blessing of the Church."

"Perhaps you prefer me to take her without benefit of clergy," Adam said icily. "Don Luis would not care to hear you suggest it."

"She is little more than a child, frightened for her life."

"A child," Adam echoed. "Your eyes have deceived you. Look for yourself. I see a woman."

Maria Elena was standing at the top of the companionway, her hair streaming behind her in the wind. Adam saw the necklace flashing at her throat and knew she wore it as a gesture of defiance to warn him that, despite her surrender, she was still a Choulqueras. He had not forgotten and he intended to treat her as one. Stepping forward, he took her by the hand and drew her to his side.

"Do you see any marks of violence on her?" he demanded of the priest.

"My dear child, I know this man has used some method of the devil to make you agree to this alliance," Father Paulus said.

"Captain MacDonald has used neither violence, nor persuasion of any kind," Maria Elena replied calmly. "To become his wife is small payment for saving not only my life, but my brother's. It is a debt of honour."

"Which can surely wait until your father can give you away with the dignity becoming your rank."

"The talk is over," Adam broke in harshly. "Will you marry us or must I stop along the coast and find another priest?"

"*Por favor*," Maria Elena whispered. "I wish it."

"The house of Choulqueras is of the Catholic faith," Father Paulus snapped.

"I, too, am of that faith. You may proceed."

The priest shrugged, beaten.

"Very well."

Maria Elena began to sway as he opened his prayer book and at once she felt the steadying pressure of Adam's hand on her arm. He did not look at her throughout the ceremony, nor attempt to touch her when it was over. There was a coldness about the whole affair which caused her fears to increase. Immediately afterwards she was escorted back to the small cabin and locked in. No Father Paulus to give her counsel, only her faithful, sympathetic Ninetta.

Late that afternoon the *Nemesis* dropped anchor and the crew set about their own wedding celebrations. To Maria Elena moving restlessly about the cabin, unable to sleep or sit down for any length of time, it was like being imprisoned in the hold of the pirate ship again. She was bound, not by metal chains but by those of wedlock, binding her to a man she both hated and feared. She had saved Manuel's life, but in doing so had committed an act which would make her an outcast in her father's eyes. He would be the laughing stock of the English court and for that he would never forgive her.

It came to her at last that Adam MacDonald had known this. It was part of his plan to bring about the downfall of her family. What the rest of it might be she could not imagine, and that frightened her more than anything.

When darkness fell, Ninetta lighted the lamps suspended from the beams strung across the ceiling and finished repacking her mistress's trousseau, tutting and complaining over the many marks made on the delicate materials by the grubby hands of the *Nemesis*' crew.

Maria Elena watched her turn back the covers on the bed and lay out a nightdress and robe of blue silk. Suddenly she became aware of what she was doing and colour flamed into her cheeks.

"Ninetta, put those things away at once. If he expects to find me waiting for him, he is mistaken and so are you."

"It will be better for him to find you in a nightdress than in nothing at all," Ninetta answered, looking at the heavy dress Maria Elena was wearing. "You cannot sleep in that."

"You are right. My head aches so, I can hardly think. Undress me, Ninetta. I pray he will not come, but if he does, I do not want him to find me like this."

Maria Elena's heart leapt as the door was unlocked, but it was Paco who entered bringing with him a tray of food.

"With the capitan's compliments." He glanced over his shoulder at Ninetta. "She is to come with me."

"I will not," Ninetta declared, moving closer to her mistress. Did he think she would sleep with him now after his part in the afternoon's work? She had seen him beside the hold, laughing and drinking and sometimes hurling insults at the man chained below.

"Go with him," Maria Elena ordered quietly. If it was Adam MacDonald's intention to leave her alone and friendless and thereby shatter what little composure remained, she was prepared.

Ninetta swept past Paco, her lips pressed tightly together in anger. Catching her by the wrist, he held her fast while he relocked the door and then he led her to the cabin where she had slept before. There was a tray of food and a bottle of wine on one of the crates.

"You must drink the health of my *capitano* and your mistress," Paco said as she stood in silence.

Crossing to the bottle, Ninetta picked it up. She turned and deliberately dropped it on the floor in front of him.

"I do not want your wine – or your kind words, they mean nothing."

"Last night you felt differently." He was looking at her in puzzlement.

"Last night my poor mistress was not married to your

hateful captain," Ninetta shouted. "He forced her to agree and you helped him! You would have killed Don Manuel."

"Are you sure your concern is not for him?"

For a moment he thought she would pick up the tray and hurl it at him.

"My lady is nearly out of her mind. She has been good to me and I cannot bear to see her so unhappy."

"And her brother?"

"I wish with all my heart he was dead. To him I am just another faceless creature to amuse him," she said and at the bitterness in her voice, Paco frowned.

"Has he touched you?" he demanded fiercely.

"Yes."

"Did you wish it?"

"I have never wanted it – with any of them, but it made no difference."

Paco's handsome face grew cold and hard as he contemplated the pain and humiliation she had endured. Nobility, Diablo! Why did God not strike them all dead? He gazed into Ninetta's tortured face and his eyes blazed.

"The others I can do nothing about," he replied, "but I swear Manuel Choulqueras will die by my hand."

The sound of the door being unlocked brought Maria Elena leaping to her feet. Adam came in and closed the door and stood for a moment staring down at the tray of untouched food.

"That was foolish. You hurt no one but yourself. Are you intending to act this way until we reach England?"

"How else would you suggest under the circumstances?" Maria Elena retorted with immense dignity.

"Despite the name you bear, which is a natural setback, I believe you to be a sensible young woman," Adam said. "Behave as one and you'll not find me completely lacking in feelings. I've good reason for the things I've done. Understand that and you have nothing to fear from me."

He was trying to win her over with soft words and kindness, Maria Elena thought in disgust.

"I find your actions contemptible, Captain MacDonald. I know my father will share my feelings when Manuel tells him how you kept him chained in the hold like a dog, fed only on water and biscuits . . ." she broke off, paling. "He – he is still alive? You promised."

"To keep him alive for the moment."

"Now I understand. He will live only as long as I behave myself. Dear God, what kind of a man are you? You condemn Sir Thomas for his women, but are you any better when it is your intention to force yourself upon me?"

The thought had not been uppermost in Adam's mind; if anything he was beginning to respect the courage she had shown and had come to tell her as much. Now, she dared to compare him with Thomas Wyndham and anger overcame his growing feeling of pity for her helplessness.

"I have heard Spanish women are well schooled in the art of being obedient," he said coldly and her cheeks grew bright with embarrassment at his bold gaze. "I hope you were attentive to your lessons."

In two long strides he covered the space between them and grasped her by the shoulders, forcing back her head to take possession of her mouth.

Maria Elena closed her eyes, faint with horror as his hands loosened her robe and pulled it from her rigid body. There was only one thought in her mind, submission. To resist would arouse his temper and he would probably take her by force anyway before slitting her brother's throat, and yet she found herself beginning to struggle, pitting all her strength against his determination to master her. The past days of bondage, of starvation and fear, had sapped her strength to the minimum and her efforts were feeble and soon overcome.

Ninetta came to awaken her mistress next morning with instructions from Adam that she was to join him in the outer cabin for breakfast. She gasped at the sight of the dark smudges on her mistress's wrists and shoulders.

"Don Luis will kill him. If he does not, I will," she vowed.

Maria Elena quickly pulled on her robe. Not since Ruy, her eldest cousin had stolen a kiss in the gardens at the Casa, in action which earned him a sound whipping from her father, and later the unpleasant incident with Thomas Wyndham, had anyone ever dared to lay hands on her.

Adam MacDonald's love-making had left her dazed and weak, for he had made no attempt to consider her feelings. He had given her a chance to submit gracefully and she had refused it, now she was to pay the penalty. She had not moved when he left her side, nor when she heard the door close behind his departing figure some while later. She had scarcely enough strength to turn her face into the pillows and cry.

"Ninetta, what is to become of me? Manuel will surely kill me when he finds out what has happened. But he was so strong – I could do nothing." She burst into a fit of weeping and fell back on to the pillows, her face in her hands.

It was an hour before Ninetta succeeded in calming her sufficiently to get her out of bed and dress her. The little maid soothed and comforted her, but there was no pity in her voice. Sadness, yes, but not pity. At a time like this nothing could dispel the hurt and shame – who knew better than Ninetta how her mistress felt?

The girl who sat opposite Adam at the breakfast table was exceedingly pale and made no attempt at conversation. She wore a dress of saffron yellow trimmed with matching lace and Ninetta had arranged her hair in a thick coil on the top of her head. But for the awful pallor and the presence of the man opposite, Maria Elena realised, she might have been sitting down to eat in her own home. The table was covered with a spotless linen cloth on which rested silver plates containing a varied assortment of delicious food. She had not eaten for the past twenty-four hours, and wondered if this was meant to tempt her. Her eyes rested on the dish full of fresh fruit, but she refrained from touching it. She only sipped at the sweet golden wine in the silver goblet at her elbow and ate nothing.

Adam glanced at her briefly when she entered and instantly returned his attention to the map on the table in front of him. She did not know that he had noticed the emerald ring still on her finger and was wondering why she had not chosen another to match the pearls at her throat. In an instant he knew, and the fingers holding the parchment tightened until the knuckles grew white. He had searched her jewel-caskets while she slept without finding any phials of poison or any rings large enough to hold a secret cavity. He had completely forgotten the ring she wore at the wedding ceremony. She would not try to use it yet, he decided, not while she believed he would kill Manuel. But later, when the ship reached England and she was faced with the prospect of having to offer up an explanation to her father, that would be the dangerous time.

For a long while after he had made love to her, he had stood by the window listening to the sound of her sobbing until eventually it had driven him from the cabin. It had affected him more than he cared to admit and his mastery of her body, though forceful, had given him pleasure such as he had not known with other women.

He had never been in love. Experience with different women over the years had taught him that an innocent face did not always portray an angel of virtue and the unfaithfulness of his mother and the deceit he had seen up and down the coast had made him hard and bitter. He had never used his strength to take a woman before. The pretended show of anger or innocence, sometimes a playful struggle, inevitably gave way to surrender.

Maria Elena had not uttered a word when he drew away from her, but he had seen a look of misery in her eyes which he knew he never wanted to see again. It had been some considerable time since Adam MacDonald had been troubled by a conscience.

Maria Elena raised her head and asked sharply, "Why?"

He selected a piece of fruit from the dish before answering, deliberating prolonging her agony.

"Because by hurting you, I hurt your father. Do you understand me?"

"The marriage – yes, but – afterwards . . ."

"You brought that on yourself," Adam returned. "You challenged my motives. I'm the kind of man who always takes up a challenge. Remember that in the future."

Maria Elena could scarcely conceal a shudder. What future did she have now? Better a quick death and an end to it all. Unconsciously her fingers strayed to the emerald ring, and her mind was made up. When Manuel was free, she would end this nightmare for ever.

"You will not escape my father's vengeance," she said. "When the Queen of England hears how you attacked a ship under her protection you will have a very hard time justifying your actions."

"Did you really think I would make a mistake at this stage of the game?" Adam declared scornfully. "We were in Spanish waters when the engagement took place and therefore the *Santa Margarita* was anyone's prize. As for our marriage, what could you tell the Queen? You married me of your own free will and as your husband I naturally exercised my rights. As for Manuel, who will believe I had him confined in chains after deliberately setting out to rescue you both? I suggest you think carefully before you make any complaint against me. You are safe, that is what will count with the Queen. A little less sure of yourself perhaps, and I like you better for it, a pity you will change again once you are returned to the bosom of your loving father."

He was openly laughing at her, Maria Elena thought.

Did he suspect the kind of reception she would receive, or was he merely enjoying her discomfort. Stiffly she rose to her feet intending to return to the bedroom, but the thought of remaining in the confinements of the small cabin suddenly made her feel ill.

"Am I allowed on deck?"

"If you wish, but I advise against it. You may hear language to which you are not accustomed."

"These past few days I have grown used to many unpleasant things," she answered and he smiled, rising to bar her way to the door.

"Don't go near your brother. He may try to persuade you to stick a knife in my back and the outcome of such stupidness would have dire results for you both.

"If only I had the courage . . ."

"You wouldn't enjoy the treatment received afterwards at the hands of my crew. They're an ill-assorted bunch from all parts of the world, and each one has his own particular brand of torture. You might last a day, no, less than that – six hours at the most."

What little colour there was in Maria Elena's cheeks ebbed slowly away at his words and her hands flew to her mouth in horror. Adam swore beneath his breath.

"Forgive me, I've tried to be gentle with you, this morning to make up for last night . . ." He broke off, watching disbelief creep into her eyes. The words had slipped out and he meant them. But he could not – he must harbour no sentimental thoughts towards this girl or he would never be able to use her against her family as he had intended. Yet there was something hauntingly beautiful about her wide, green eyes. They had such depth of colour and betrayed her every thought.

"Maria Elena . . ." He used her name for the first time and stepped close to her, his hands reaching out to grasp her by the shoulders.

She swayed against him, her senses numb with shock. He wanted her and she was helpless to refuse him. She bore his kisses in a tortured silence, aware of an overwhelming desire to surrender herself completely to this passionate man who had taken her by storm.

The door opened slowly and noiselessly behind him. Maria Elena saw the knife first, a wicked-looking dagger with a long curved blade plunging down towards her husband's back and she screamed. Why, when his death would have both freed her from a loathsome marriage and avenged her stolen honour, she did not know.

Adam wheeled about seizing her by the arms as he did so and throwing her bodily across the far side of the room. As she reeled back against the window, Maria Elena saw the dirty, bearded face of the man closing with Adam, the knife between them. The eyes were wild with madness and she had seen that look before, when her brother had whipped a stable boy to death because he had forgotten to feed his favourite stallion.

The two men fell to the floor, rolling towards her in a flurry of arms and legs while she prayed desperately for her brother to find enough strength to overcome Adam MacDonald and undo the harm she had brought about. But it was her brother who lay still on the floor and her husband who rose to his feet, the knife in his hand. A scream escaped her lips at the sight of the blood on the blade.

"You've killed him."

She fell on her knees beside Manuel and cradled his head in her lap. She did not hear Adam open the door and shout for his first mate or hear his instructions for Manuel to be taken to Abel Black's cabin and the guard on duty, given three lashes for allowing him to escape. When men crowded into the cabin and tried to take him from her, she screamed at them hysterically in Spanish and pushed them away.

Adam bent over her and lifted her up, imprisoning both her wrists in one hand, while the other gripped the back of her neck and forced her head up.

"If you continue to struggle, I'll knock you cold."

The threat took immediate effect. She stood dishevelled and panting in his grasp while Manuel was removed from the cabin.

"You can't put him back in the hold . . ."

"He's going to my first mate's cabin. There is no doctor on board, your maid will have to look after him."

Maria Elena sagged against him, her senses reeling, and for a moment she experienced total blackness. When it passed she found herself in a chair, with Adam still supporting her.

"Drink this."

He put a glass to her lips and she drank the wine without argument. He released her and stepped back frowning.

"You thought he was dead? Didn't you see the wound was only in the shoulder?"

Mutely she shook her head. Adam filled the glass she had used and took a long drink.

"If you hadn't screamed – I owe you my life," he said harshly.

"And you saved me from the pirates." She stood up. "I want to go to my brother."

"Paco is outside. He will take you."

He turned away from her to stare bleakly out of the window and did not watch her leave.

CHAPTER FIVE

"You little fool," Manuel said coldly and slapped Maria Elena hard across the face. The sound hung in the stillness of the cabin like a pistol shot. She fell to the floor, holding her hand to a smarting cheek.

"I'm sorry, I only saw the knife. I was afraid. Manuel – please don't be angry."

"But for you he would be dead."

"And so would we, he said so." Maria Elena bit her lips fiercely. The dreaded moment had come. "Manuel, I am his wife."

"I know. The fool guarding me got drunk and talked his head off. For once you showed remarkable good sense."

She could hardly believe her ears. No anger, no reproaches, not even a word of consolation or gratitude for her sacrifice. As long as he had his life, he cared little what it had cost. her.

"It will not be difficult to have the marriage annulled. Father Paulus will testify you had pressure brought to bear on you and I, of course, will appear the most devoted of brothers, eager to have my poor sister freed from a monster." Manuel looked into her distraught features and smiled cruelly. "If you look like that the Queen will be in tears before the hearing is over."

"Stop it, stop laughing at me! I won't be treated like a child. I am not any longer, Adam MacDonald saw to that. Don't you understand, Manuel, there can be no annulment." The anger vanished and she bowed her head as her brother raised himself on one elbow, scowling. "I am truly his wife."

"Our father will kill you," he told her, his voice a harsh whisper. "If I do not do it first."

"Will he? Why, we are both alive? The alternative was your death. Have I acted so wrongly?"

Her brother did not answer and Maria Elena rose to her feet in silent contempt. He could not condemn her because he was a coward. Wordlessly she moved towards the door.

"You have brought dishonour on our name," Manuel sneered. "But what can be expected with the watery blood of an Englishwoman in your veins? She was weak, too. You are like her, sister. Weak and vulnerable."

With a strong wind to aid her, the *Nemesis* made good time on the return journey. At the end of the sixth day, they were in sight of the Dover coast.

"We reach our mooring tomorrow afternoon," Adam said to Maria Elena as they sat at dinner that evening. "Paco will go ahead to the house and send back a carriage for us."

"House?"

She looked up from her dessert in surprise. She had supposed he would take her directly to the Palace. It had been easy to forget that she was his wife these past days. He had not been near her and had conveyed messages through Ninetta whenever necessary. She mostly ate alone, walked alone on deck, always late in the evening and watched over by Paco and slept alone.

"Near St. James's."

His eyes rested momentarily on her pale face. She looked tired and drawn and her appetite had not improved. She ate enough to keep her alive and no more. Since the day Manuel had been wounded she had not returned to his cabin and Adam often wondered what had passed between them.

"Is Manuel to go with us?" she asked. "I won't speak to the Queen if you allow him to live. I – I will even go on being – being your wife, if you wish it."

His eyes were on her face, probing mercilessly. Maria Elena blushed and glanced away, hating herself for being so nervous. Did he suspect she meant to take her life once her brother was free?

"Why not? I could get used to having a wife around and I have no doubt Manuel and I will meet again before very long."

"You really hate us, don't you? Why? Tell me, I beg of you."

Adam's mouth tightened. With slow deliberation he folded his napkin and laid it to one side, lost for a moment in thoughts she knew nothing about and probably never would.

"Luis Choulqueras is responsible for my father's death," he said at length. "My mother was also his mistress until he discarded her and tossed her into the gutter."

"I do not believe you! My father loved my mother, he never looked at another woman," Maria Elena gasped.

"That isn't the truth and you know it. Manuel's mother was a *gitana* girl. Your mother was English. I admit he married her, but there were always others, before and after."

Maria Elena sat in a stunned silence as he told her of the various women with whom her father had been associated. she knew instinctively that it was true and his tone of voice – the half-smile on his face – was an added incentive to believe. Now she understood why her mother had rarely smiled or laughed, and why her nerves were continually frayed. Near to her death she had become an invalid, confined to bed and for ever plagued with nightmares. Maria Elena realised she had known of her husband's infidelity and yet no word of reproach had passed her lips. Had she been afraid of him as her daughter was of Manuel?

Adam MacDonald's words returned to haunt Maria

Elena that night and to disturb her sleep long after Ninetta had tucked her into bed and left her alone. The open window allowed a cool breeze to penetrate the otherwise stuffy cabin and at length she got up to sit on the window seat and stare at the sea in a miserable silence. Tomorrow the *Nemesis* docked at Wapping and tomorrow her husband would flaunt his victory before her father. She shuddered to think of the outcome. She had wrecked her father's plans and that was unpardonable.

She began to shiver and stood up as the door opened. Adam came in. Had he come to instruct her how to behave when they arrived at court? she wondered.

His gaze wandered over the beautiful damask silk nightgown she wore, the neckline and sleeves heavily embroidered with lace.

"Are all your things packed?"

"Yes."

"You don't seem over anxious to be re-united with your father."

Maria Elena thought he sounded sorry for the predicament he had placed her in and wondered what would happen if she broke down and cried in front of him as she sorely wanted to. In time she remembered she was a Choulqueras and she did not ask for mercy from an enemy.

"My father will kill you," she said coldly. "He will have you roasted alive, drawn and quartered – and I will watch. Do you hear? I want to watch you die."

Her head went back defiantly as he stepped towards her his face growing dark and seized her by the shoulders. She winced, but did not cry out. Whatever he did to her she would not complain, nor would she give way to tears again. Soon she would be free of him.

"I think you realise I can break you as easily as I'd break a twig of heather."

"And you'd get great pleasure from it, Captain MacDonald, would you not?"

A frown creased Adam's face. He held her at arms' length and stared at her intently. The defiance which blazed from her eyes stirred him to admiration.

"Why do you fight me?" he demanded. "Am I so ugly, my body so deformed you can't stand to look at me? My God, I'm twice the man you think Thomas Wyndham to be."

"You dare to ask me why, when you have taken me by force and hold the threat of my brother's death over my head!"

"I give you your brother's life," Adam said harshly. "I'm man enough to take what I want without that kind of help."

Maria Elena was pale and trembling, mostly with anger, but also pain. The grip on her shoulders was making her feel exceedingly faint.

"You are an animal. I hate you." She spat the words at him furiously.

"Then you must expect me to act like one," he said between set teeth. "And as you prefer force . . ."

He lifted her on to the bed and plied her mouth with kisses far more passionate than any Maria Elena had endured so far. Her attempts to remain unaroused by his demands were thwarted by the kisses he forced on her mouth until it was no longer unwilling, and her trembling body conceded to the every wish of his experienced hands. When he drew away from her she was horrified to find she did not want to cry as before. The realisation that he was master not only of her body, but of her soul too, was enough to make her move as far away from him as was possible and hide her burning cheeks in the pillows.

The *Nemesis* dropped anchor a little before noon the following day. Paco left immediately for the house to acquaint Jamie MacDonald of the arrival of an unexpected guest.

It was a bitterly cold day and snow was falling heavily. Maria Elena sat in her cabin in a state of nerves. She was shivering, despite the warm ermine lined cloak she wore over a thick travelling dress, and Ninetta had refused to go with Paco to supervise the preparation of her apartments. Maria Elena had not the heart to scold her, but she sent her to the house anyway, not wishing her husband to know that she needed moral support of any kind.

For an hour she had been watching the gang-plank, waiting to see her brother leave the ship, but so far there had been no sign of him. She was debating whether or not to tackle Adam when the door opened and Manuel pushed past the guard outside to stand before his sister.

"Leave us," he snapped at the sailor. "And don't listen at the door."

"So he has kept his word," Maria Elena breathed. "Did you bargain with him again?"

"Yes."

Manuel was dressed in seaman's clothes, borrowed from one of the crew and there was a week's growth of beard on his chin. The sling Ninetta had put on his arm had been discarded and it now hung limply by his side.

"You don't look like an outraged woman," he said, eyeing her appearance. "You have obviously found him a satisfactory lover."

"Everything I have done, has been for your sake," his sister replied quietly.

"I am not in the mood to fall on my knees and kiss the hem of your skirt," Manuel flung back. Had she really expected him to be grateful? "Our father will expect a better explanation than that."

"You need have no fear people will laugh at you behind your back." Maria Elena's hands locked tightly together and the hard emerald ring cut into her palm. "I know what I must do."

"It's too late for that now. I have thought of a way to turn this whole incident to our advantage." He stepped closer to her, his glittering eyes riveted on her ashen face.

"I have but a moment, or the man outside will get suspicious. You will go with MacDonald and you will do everything he asks of you. If necessary pretend you are taken with him. You have been well trained so you should not find it difficult. Besides, he finds you attractive or he would not have slept with you again. You have hidden talent, my dear, now is the time to bring it into the open and use it on Adam MacDonald."

The blood drained from Maria Elena's face. Death – yes, she had been prepared for that and willing to die, but to surrender herself to the arms of a man she hated and pretend it was of her own choosing . . .

"No Manuel, no. You do not know what you ask."

Her brother's hands closed over her bandaged wrists, tightening until she cried out in pain.

"You can and you will do it. If MacDonald kills me – or Father, he will throw you into the street because he will have no further use for you. No man will look at you after his hands have despoiled you. Your one chance is to help us have our revenge on him and in doing so prove you have a little Choulqueras blood in you."

"I – I can't." Maria Elena's voice grew shrill with pain as he forced her slowly to her knees. "Yes, yes, I will do it."

"Fail me in this and you will wish you had never been born," he hissed.

Sick and giddy Maria Elena stood massaging her bruised wrists as he flung open the door and strode out, almost cannoning into someone directly outside. She heard a sharp exchange of words before Adam stepped into the cabin. One brief glance at her was enough to tell him Manuel had said more than goodbye.

"Are you ill?" His eyes darted from her face to the red marks just above the bandages on her wrists.

"I – I felt faint. I fell," Maria Elena stammered. It was not a very convincing lie and she knew he did not believe her.

"If you're cold, we'll go across the river and have a hot toddy," he said as she shivered.

It was only a short journey to the tavern, but by the time the small open boat drew alongside the landing stage, a cutting wind had chilled Maria Elena to the bone. Adam lifted her out and ushered her quickly up the narrow wooden Pelican Stairs hugging the side of the tavern and through a side door into the tap room. He felt her hang back at the sight of the curious faces turning in their direction, but he ignored it and beckoned forward a serving girl.

"Is there a room free?"

"At the top of the stairs, Capt'n." The girl knew him from previous visits, but she had never known him to bring a woman with him before. She stared at Maria Elena, amused that she was brazen enough to appear without her face hidden. It was not unusual for the nobility to come and go from the rooms upstairs. She had seen many discreetly cloaked ladies arriving late at night and departing before morning.

"Bring a bottle of whisky and a hot drink for the lady," Adam ordered.

The girl watched them climb the stairs before turning towards the kitchens, stopping to pass a lewd comment on the new arrivals as she did so.

"Bessie."

"Yes, ma'am."

The Duchess came out of the Aft Cabin where she had waited for Adam to go upstairs.

"You were told to fetch drinks."

"He won't mind waiting a while," the girl answered carelessly. "It'll give him a chance to get better acquainted with his lady friend. Did you get a load o' those sparklers? Lordy, the capt'n's on to a good thing this time."

"You stupid little fool, get to the kitchens before I box your ears. I'll attend to Captain MacDonald myself. Bring me the silver tray and a bottle of the best whisky."

"Fancy him then, do you?" Bessie asked cheekily.

She shrieked with laughter as the older woman pushed past her and went into the parlour.

When she entered the room upstairs, the Duchess found Maria Elena seated in one of the booths against the wall, still wearing her snow-covered cloak. She looked petrified with cold. There was no fire in the room, only a table and two chairs and a four-poster bed. The people who visited these rooms did not usually come for comfort. Adam turned from the window and his face broke into a mocking smile at the sight of her.

"Duchess! I'm flattered."

Sarah MacDonald put down the tray on the white scrubbed table in front of Maria Elena.

"The lady looks half frozen. Why don't you let her sit downstairs by the fire?"

"The lady is the daughter of Don Luis Choulqueras and hardly accustomed to sitting with the likes of the rabble below," Adam answered dryly. "Besides, we shall not be here long . My carriage is coming to collect us."

Maria Elena was aware of a pair of hazel eyes raking her from head to toe, not with the same mild interest as when the woman had first come in, but with an intentness that was almost frightening, and for a moment there was something disturbingly familiar about her.

"Ah, yes, the illustrious Luis Choulqueras!" the Duchess exclaimed quietly, and once more the heavily-powdered face was masked by a smile. "The whole of London has been awaiting your return, captain."

"How the devil did anyone know where I was going . . ." Adam began and then he remembered he had left Caroline in his house. She would not have kept his secret for long.

"Don Luis was of the opinion you had sailed, not to effect a rescue, but to ensure that neither his daughter nor son returned alive."

And if only you had, Sarah thought bitterly. She had

seen Manuel leave the *Nemesis* and had prayed the gangplank would collapse and hurl him into the icy waters of the Thames. As for his sister – Sarah stared down at the silent girl with mixed feelings and wondering what Adam was up to.

His vows of vengeance against the house of Choulqueras were well known to her. The crew of the *Nemesis* talked freely in her company, especially when the ale was free and plentiful and there was also her continued association with Jamie MacDonald. He had not forgotten that she had saved his life when Luis Choulqueras had the torch put to the MacDonald house, and although he had not forgiven her the betrayal of his master, he relented sufficiently to send news of her son's whereabouts from time to time.

Adam finished his second glass of whisky and Sarah refilled it. He could not hold his liquor, like his father, she liked to watch a man who could drink and not get drunk. Luis Choulqueras drank only wine, but then he was not a man. She could not think of a word vile enough to describe the inhuman monster who had tossed her aside when he was tired of her.

When the Duchess had gone and she was alone with Adam again, Maria Elena looked up from her hot toddy and asked, "Manuel has gone to our father. You know they will go directly to the Queen?"

Adam did not look in the least perturbed and her anxiety increased. "You will be arrested at once. If she does not have your head my father will demand satisfaction—" Her voice trailed off in horror and a look of fear crossed her face. "You did not use me merely to hurt my father, this is what you really wanted . . . a duel. He is master of both pistol and sword. He will kill you." She said the words with conviction, but even as she uttered them she began to wonder.

"We shall see," Adam murmured.

Maria Elena's glance fell to the poison ring she wore. It

would be so easy to slip the powder into her drink. She would be dead within a matter of seconds. Trembling, she began to draw it from her finger, but just then a lean brown hand plucked it from her grasp and she looked up to see it disappearing into a pocket in her husband's leather doublet.

"Give it back to me," she cried.

"You're no use to me dead," Adam said cruelly.

"How long have you known?"

"That you intended to take you own life? The first time I saw the ring on your finger. Did you think Spanish women are the only ones to own such pretty ornaments of destruction? You've been contemplating killing yourself since you fell into my hands; your code demands it, more so now than before. Was Manuel giving you a subtle reminder earlier?"

"No, You mustn't think that." She broke off in confusion She was unaccustomed to continual lies and deceit and sought desperately for an answer to satisfy him without giving away the new role Manuel had thrust upon her. She looked at him calmly despite the wild beating of her heart "It is likely a duel will result whether I am alive or dead. I would have killed myself, but now I think perhaps I am glad you stopped me. These past days I have discovered that the word honour covers a multitude of sins. It would be senseless to end my life because I have been taught it is the thing to do."

Was she trying to intimate she was willing to go on being his wife? Adam wondered. A suggestion like that would most certainly have come from Manuel. The last night aboard the *Nemesis* she had fought him like a tigress, which was not the action of a woman about to concede defeat.

"Is there some kind of celebration going on?" Maria Elena asked, staring out of the carriage window at the crowds of people milling through the streets. Earlier they had passed a group of mummers surrounded by an amused audience, and now she could see men and women dancing.

"A fair, perhaps," Adam suggested, but he knew it was not. He had heard the news as they left the tavern and was silently shocked. How was Jamie MacDonald taking the terrible news that the Queen of Scotland had been found guilty of treason and was to be executed?

Maria Elena was still intrigued by the revellers. How would she take it, and her father too? If there were to be reprisals over the unfortunate Mary's death, he would be involved. What a perfect opportunity to send the fleet of ships he had seen at Cadiz.

The carriage came to a halt before the house and there was Jamie MacDonald, his weatherbeaten face impassive as he helped Maria Elena to alight.

"Welcome, Mistress MacDonald. I am Jamie, the master's steward," he said escorting her inside, with Adam following close behind. "I've had rooms prepared for ye on the first floor if ye'd care to inspect them."

"My wife will find them satisfactory," Adam said flatly.

Maria Elena ignored the veiled threat and made her way upstairs. Jamie MacDonald followed Adam into the study and closed the door behind them.

"The lass looks as if she's had a rough voyage," he muttered. He tried not to sound concerned, but the pale face of the beautiful girl he had just seen possessed the innocence of an angel and he was taken aback. He had been expecting an older woman with a closer resemblance to Luis Choulqueras, not a reed-slender girl with a quiet dignity which had immediately commanded his respect.

"There is fire beneath the ice," Adam drawled. "Don't let her fool you into believing otherwise."

"In the name of heaven, what made you marry her?"

"I've deprived Don Luis of something he loves."

"Ye will have a hard time explaining it to the Queen, especially with the *Santa Margarita* a week overdue. He swears you sailed to intercept her."

"He's right. Her cargo is in the hold of the *Nemesis*. You'd better expect Paco after midnight."

"Wasn't there supposed to be a priest on board?"

"Father Paulus." Adam chuckled. "Don't look so worried, I haven't damned my soul to the eternal fires by killing him. He performed the wedding. Faith, I'd like to hear him trying to explain it to Don Luis. If Manuel doesn't slit his throat, he'll end up in some alley with a knife in his back." Adam relaxed into a chair with a heavy sigh, feeling easier now he was home. He was master of his house and his wife too if she challenged his authority. With the Spaniard so near at hand to revive old wounds, he would not again be troubled by the lapses of sentimentality he had experienced on board the *Nemesis*.

"Pour me a drink, Jamie, and I'll tell you what I'm up to. And afterwards I want to know everything that has happened while I was away."

Adam sent word to Maria Elena to be ready to leave the house at seven that evening. The Queen had graciously granted them an audience at eight o'clock. He wondered what her reaction had been to the five chests of treasure he had had delivered secretly to the palace and if, despite her apparent change of attitude, Maria Elena might not make a complaint against him after all.

There was no sign of the pale, nervous girl he had grown accustomed to when he met her at the bottom of the stairs that evening. He was confronted by an elegantly groomed young woman, poised and disturbingly attractive. Her dress was of green silk, embroidered with pearls. Maria Elena knew she had to look like a bride lest the Queen grew suspicious, and then she would not be able to carry out Manuel's instructions.

"Will you help me with this, please."

She held out her cloak and Adam slipped it around her shoulders in silence. She lifted her hands to fasten the silver clasp at her throat and he saw that the bandages on her wrists had been discarded and the skin carefully treated with powder to hide the ugly bruises which still remained. The marks brought to mind Manuel's visit to her cabin and his suspicions increased. He would do well to be on his guard for the remainder of the evening.

"We will be late," Adam said as Jamie closed the door of the carriage behind them. "Send the servants to bed before Paco arrives."

The steward nodded understandingly and motioned to the driver to proceed. Maria Elena was aware she was under close scrutiny throughout the short drive to the Palace, but she said nothing and not once did she glance at her husband.

A servant took them directly to Elizabeth's private sitting room, where they found the Queen surrounded by her ladies-in-waiting. Adam had a brief glimpse of Caroline Stacey rising from her seat before she left the room with her companions.

As soon as they were alone, Elizabeth stretched out her hand towards Adam and he went down on one knee before her and kissed the heavily ringed fingers.

"Pray do not stand on ceremony, good Captain. I am well pleased with you, but there are those who are not. I fear for your safety if Don Luis presents me with a formal complaint."

The Queen raised her head and stared at the girl behind him. Here was the only raincloud in the clear sky.

"Don't be afraid, girl, I won't bite," she said suddenly. It was a remark characteristic of her father and was accompanied by the same disarming smile. Maria Elena came forward and swept down into an elaborate curtsey. "My dear child, you have no idea how relieved I am to see you safe and well." Elizabeth bent forward and taking her by the hand, raised her to her feet. "Let me look at you. A little pale and thin, but that's to be expected after your terrible ordeal. You were not harmed?"

"No, Your Majesty, they intended holding me for ransom."

"What have we here?" The Queen was staring down at the thick gold wedding band on the girl's left hand. She raised incredulous eyes to meet Adam's bland stare. The young rogue had gone too far this time. Wedded to the Spaniard's daughter? He would have a fit.

Maria Elena felt the colour mounting slowly in her cheeks. Her position was so humiliating she wished the floor would open and swallow her up. She dared not look at Adam.

He stepped forward, the smile on his face masking a moment of uneasiness. Maria Elena's silence did not perturb him; he had merely underestimated her courage and loyalty to her family, but why had her father or brother not been waiting to challenge him the moment he arrived in the palace?

"The señorita and I were married at sea."

"A love match!" Elizabeth exclaimed.

She had never considered Thomas Wyndham a suitable husband for this beautiful child and had begun to suspect an ulterior motive for Don Luis' choice. Adam MacDonald and Maria Elena Choulqueras, the daughter of his enemy. It was like holding a torch to a keg of gunpowder.

"What else, Your Majesty?" Adam murmured.

Maria Elena's colour heightened and she quickly lowered her gaze, hearing the faint note of mockery in his tone that Elizabeth missed and knowing it was directed at her. She could not have given a more convincing portrayal of a shy young bride.

Elizabeth placed the girl's hand in Adam's, her eyes twinkling. Now was not the time to probe too depply; she would wait and watch.

"You have both my approval and my blessing and you, Captain MacDonald, also have my deepest thanks for what you did. Had you not put to sea so promptly this child would have become something far less pleasant than a bride and those other poor people – my people, would have ended their days in misery." Elizabeth's gaze moved from his face to someone who had just entered behind him and Adam saw the corners of her mouth tighten. "Don Luis, don't linger by the door. Come, welcome your daughter home."

CHAPTER SIX

THE tall figure of Luis Choulqueras bowed low before the Queen he hated so much. He still retained the Spanish custom of wearing black, and he presented a formidable sight.

"Your Majesty, I came as soon as I heard the good news."

"You liar, Adam thought. Manuel had reached the palace at least seven hours ago. Time enough for anger to pass and plans to be made. A glove thrown in his face as he arrived; a hired assassin with a knife for his back – yet nothing had so far happened. Adam realised he was to be played at his own game and Maria Elena was involved up to her pretty little neck. A sudden wave of hot anger swept over him and he felt inclined to teach her a lesson she would not forget.

Don Luis turned and embraced his daughter.

"Manuel has told me everything. You have had a terrible experience."

Over her shoulder his hate-filled eyes met Adam's. *You will die slowly and in great agony for this*, they said.

"Father, are you not angry?" Maria Elena whispered amazed.

"Angry, *niña*? You have repaid a debt of honour. It is what I would have expected of you."

"This is no debt of honour, but a love match," Elizabeth murmured. "The way Captain MacDonald went to the rescue of your daughter despite the bad feeling between you is highly commendable. And then to fall in love – I find it most romantic," she laughed.

"Perhaps the captain would care to explain why he sank the *Santa Margarita*?"

Elizabeth's smile disappeared at the anger in the Spaniard's tone. Damn the man's impertinence! Adam MacDonald did not look worried, though. For him and for her, it had been a profitable encounter. The man was an incorrigible rogue; if only there were more like him.

"The *Santa Margarita* opened fire on my ship first," Adam said in level tones. "Confirmation of this has surely been given by the priest, Father Paulus. I'd hardly engage another vessel when I had the safety of my passengers to consider."

"And the men you slaughtered?"

"Were my men to lay aside their weapons and be cut down? It was unfortunate – but . . ." He shrugged meaningly.

"Under the circumstances Captain MacDonald cannot be held responsible," Elizabeth said coldly.

"With Your Majesty's permission I would like a few words with my daughter."

"You have my leave."

Luis Choulqueras took Maria Elena's arm and drew her out of earshot.

"Father –"

"*Silencio*, it is too late for excuses. I could have killed you with my bare hands when I heard you had married him. You little fool, a man like that would have been content merely to sleep with you! An addition to your dowry would have silenced any complaints from Wyndham, but no, you have to ruin months of planning with your stupidity. Wyndham was to have given support to our cause and he began talking of withdrawing both men and money when he heard. If that happens, Maria Elena, I shall deal with you personally. MacDonald finds you attractive, Manuel tells me, is it true?"

"No – no, he used me to hurt you and for no other

reason. He wanted you to be angry enough to challenge him to a duel."

"The young pup's time will come, but not yet. The next few weeks are vital to my plans and there must be no hint of scandal – nothing to provoke talk. Until I tell you otherwise, you will continue to amuse MacDonald."

"Yes, Father," Maria Elena said meekly. Argument was useless, and since Adam had enlightened her as to her father's various women, her fear of him had grown.

"If you are sensible the time will soon pass. When Philip's plans are realised I will deal with MacDonald and you will marry Sir Thomas as originally planned. I have told him you are desolate over this marriage and long for the moment when you can be with him."

"But it isn't true," Maria Elena gasped. "I hate him. He is a despicable spineless creature."

"You will not question me again," Don Luis growled, and led her back to where Adam and the Queen were deep in conversation. His face impassive, he placed his daughter's hand in Adam's. "Maria Elena has convinced me my fears were groundless," he said suavely. "Take her – and my blessing on you both."

To Maria Elena, the blessing fell on her ears like a curse.

It was after midnight when they returned to the house in St. James's. She went straight to her room, not remembering until she found the rooms in darkness that she had told Ninetta not to wait up for her.

The large double doors in her sitting room which had been locked when she tried them earlier, swung open as she stumbled in the process of searching for a candle and Adam stood there, holding a candelabrum. He stared at the dying embers of the fire and frowned in annoyance.

"The servants should have made it up before going to bed. The one in my bedroom is still alight, come and thaw out."

He turned back into his own room and Maria Elena knew it was an order, not a request. Now she would know whether or not she had the courage to carry out further deception.

He closed the doors behind her, took her cloak and tossed it across a chair, before following her to the cheerful flames crackling in the hearth.

"Why did you remain silent?" he asked after a long silence had ensued between them.

"To have done otherwise would have placed my father's life in jeopardy."

"The prospect of being my wife no longer appals you, then?" The sneer in his voice spurred her to anger and she bit her lip to suppress a cutting retort. "Does the animal no longer frighten you?"

She lifted her eyes to his dark face, her voice very controlled as she said.

"It was my father's intention to marry me to Sir Thomas, as you know. I was not consulted. I would have married him and been a good wife because I have been brought up to please my husband. Tell me, Captain Mac-Donald, if you were not blinded by hate, would you find me attractive?"

Adam winced inwardly. He had been waiting for this moment and hoping it never came.

"Captain MacDonald could never forget, but Adam, your husband, finds you both attractive and desirable. Does that please you?"

"Yes, my husband, it does."

Maria Elena could hardly believe she had spoken with such honesty; it was as if another person had uttered the words. She was not aware of him moving towards her, only of the tremendous strength of his arms as they closed around her and the hunger within her which demanded to be satisfied. His mouth closed over hers in a wild kiss that fired her blood to an uncontrollable response and made her senses reel.

When they came apart she was trembling from head to toe with the passion he had roused in her. Adam's face was cold as he stared down into her wide eyes.

"I've kissed experts at the game of deception," he scathed. "Did you really believe you were capable of fooling me?"

"You don't understand—" Maria Elena's voice was little more than a whisper. Surely he must realise there had been no pretence about her response?

"I understand only too well. When I have you it'll be on my terms, not your father's, and you won't have any say in the matter." He turned away from her and moved towards the door before delivering the final, cruellest taunt of all. "You're a child, not a woman, and I shall never find you pleasing. It was curiosity that brought me to your bed, nothing more."

Maria Elena stood swaying unsteadily before the closed door, listening to his footsteps echo on the hard wooden floor as he went downstairs and then she sank slowly into a chair, numb with shock. Not because of his anger, his words had flowed over her head and not reached her. She knew she should hate him for the way he had so cruelly violated her and had tried desperately to do so, but it was no longer possible. She was a woman; she had become one as he held her in his arms and awakened emotions deep inside her that she knew she ought not to feel.

Adam MacDonald made his own laws, obeyed his own ruthless passions and was capable of hatred such as she had never believed possible. All her disciplined upbringing had never prepared her for an encounter with such a man. He laughed at her anger, mocked her fears and undermined her confidence until common sense told her it was senseless to fight him further. He would cause her pain without caring one iota. It was better to submit to his domination as she had once willed herself to accept the marriage to Thomas Wyndham.

It would not be as difficult. Whereas the latter's caresses

had brought instant revulsion, it needed only a look from Adam to rock the ground beneath her feet. Her traitorous body had allowed itself to be awakened by his man, and she knew now that she would remain with him whatever the future held for them, for not only did she belong to Adam MacDonald – she loved him.

Maria Elena did not see him for three days. The prospect of facing him after her humilating defeat proved too much, and she remained in her apartments. Secretly she hoped he would seek her out on some pretext, but as the days passed with interminable slowness, she grew to realise that he had no intention of doing so.

Ninetta unwittingly let slip the secret of the woman Adam visited regularly at the palace as she was helping Maria Elena to dress one morning. She immediately dissolved into tears upon realising her mistress was ignorant of the liaison.

"Stop crying and tell me who she is," Maria Elena demanded. "Is she beautiful – rich?"

"It is one of the Queen's ladies-in-waiting, a Caroline Stacey. Paco says they are old friends."

"Are you still associating with that young cut-throat? I forbid you to see him again," Maria Elena snapped. She was irritable these days, losing her temper at the slightest provocation.

"He has asked me to marry him," Ninetta whispered. "I love him."

"Love! What do you know of love? He'll discard you like all the rest when he's finished with you." Maria Elena's anger dissolved as she saw fresh tears gathering in the girl's eyes. Contritely she took her in her arms. "I did not mean it, I know how you feel. I, too, am in love, only I have no hope of it ever being returned."

"With – with him?"

Maria Elena smiled faintly at Ninetta's astonishment.

"Yes, with him. He has scorned me and gone to another

woman. Take care that the same thing does not happen to you."

Ninetta was silent, thinking of the happy hours she had spent with Paco the previous evening. He came every night to her little room at the back of the house, always very late at night when the other servants were in bed and there was no chance of him being seen. Only Jamie MacDonald, who left the side door open for him and Adam knew of his presence. They had lain close together on her narrow bed, his body curled around hers lovingly, protectingly. He had said he loved her, whispering it into her ear as if he was afraid of her reaction. He was not like the others who had taken her for amusement only. He was kind and gentle and so patient, teaching her to respond, not out of habit, but became her body demanded it. She had not drawn away from him, but turned in his arms and buried her face against his chest and blurted out her own confession of love.

Ninetta looked at Maria Elena and was sad because she would never know the ecstasy of loving a man and being loved in return.

So he had gone back to an old mistress, Maria Elena thought despondently, and he was making no attempt to hide it from her. No doubt he expected her to remain indoors afraid of the gossip, and that was exactly what she had been doing. On an impulse she took her courage in her hands and decided to go out. She sent Ninetta to arrange for a carriage and selected a warm gown to wear.

Halfway down the stairs she came face to face with Jamie MacDonald. She had been waiting some considerable time for the carriage and it had not appeared.

"Are ye going out, mistress?" he asked, eyeing her attire.

"Yes, for a drive. Where is the carriage I ordered?"

"It's been sent back to the stables."

Maria Elena clutched at the stair rail for support, seeing the hostility in his eyes and hearing the faint ring of insolence in his voice. How dare he presume to question her orders?

"You forget who I am. As your master's wife, I demand courtesy from my servants and I expect my orders to be obeyed. And you will not address me as 'mistress' again or I'll have you dismissed . . ."

"Jamie, leave us," an authoritative voice ordered and as the steward moved past her, she looked down and saw Adam standing below in the main hall.

"Come down," he snapped. "Or must I give the servants the added pleasure of hearing you scream as I drag you down?"

Maria Elena swept down the stairs and into the drawing-room, determined to retain her composure, but as she turned and saw the fury blazing out of his eyes, she felt her legs grow weak. If only she had not made herself so vulnerable by falling in love with him!

"How dare you speak to Jamie in that fashion? He's served my family for over thirty years, he's no scullery lad to be scolded over some trivial matter. You'll apologise to him."

"I ordered a carriage and he sent it away," Maria Elena protested. "I had every right to reprimand him."

"Beneath my roof, you have no rights. Your position here is less than that of the lowest servant." Adam advanced towards her, his temper aggravated by her haughty manner. "Perhaps I don't make myself clear. The servants have instructions to refer all your orders to me, that's why your carriage was sent back to the stables. You'll leave this house when I permit it and not before. Where were you going, anyway? To hatch another little plot with your illustrious father?"

"I – I don't know what you mean," Maria Elena stammered.

"If you lie to me you'll not see the outside of this house for a month," Adam threatened.

"You are not concerned I will see my father, but that I

may learn of your mistress," Maria Elena flung back in equally angry tones. "I already know about her. Who she is – and what she is."

"She's a titled lady and most accommodating," her husband sneered. "We've been friends for many years, and I see no reason to discontinue our relationship merely because I have taken a wife."

"With the indifference you would take a whore," Maria Elena said and fought to hold back a rush of tears. *Dear God*, she prayed, *don't let me break down now*.

Adam smiled sardonically. At last she understood her position.

"As you say, with the indifference I would take a whore."

"Perhaps if you were to pay me for my services I might give better satisfaction."

Maria Elena saw his hand moving towards her too late. The blow rocked her on her heels and brought the tears flowing down her cheeks. Wordlessly she picked up her skirts and fled from the room.

She was breakfasting in her sitting-room as usual when Adam came in unannounced and voiced his intention of having breakfast with her. She had scarcely seen him since the day he had stuck her, two long weeks ago. She gave him no more than a cursory glance, but his presence in the chair opposite unnerved her and after a few moments she pushed away her plate.

"You'll need to eat more than that if you intend going out today," he remarked coolly.

Maria Elena looked up with a soft exclamation.

"I'll be away for most of the day supervising repairs aboard the *Nemesis*," he continued. "You may use the carriage if you wish."

"It is too cold to go out," Maria Elena said.

"It's up to you."

He finished his breakfast and left her without speaking

another word. She waited until she heard him leave the house, then called Ninetta to lay out a change of clothes. She would call on her father and beg him to send her back to Spain on the first available ship.

"What do you mean, he knows?" Manuel Choulqueras demanded. He bent over his sister and caught her chin in fingers of steel, forcing her head back. "Answer me."

"I tried, truly, but I am not used to that kind of thing," Maria Elena said wearily. "I did not deceive him for one moment."

She was wishing she had not come to her father's apartments in the palace. Manuel was with him, and Sir Thomas Wyndham, looking fatter and more ridiculous than before.

"Father, send me home," she pleaded.

"You will stay here and do as you are told," Manuel growled.

"Gently, my son, your sister is naturally upset. Adam MacDonald is a formidable opponent and we both know that he is not above humiliating his own wife in order to satisfy his own twisted sense of revenge." Luis Choulqueras came and stood beside Maria Elena's chair. "It is quite possible that I shall not wait until our plans have been realised to kill him. You have been obedient and patient, my child, and you deserve to be free."

"Then you are sending me home?"

"Home! Of course not. Adam MacDonald will be disposed of and you will go to your rightful husband."

Maria Elena stared across at Thomas Wyndham, and the look in his eyes made her feel ill.

"Adam is my rightful husband, in the eyes of God and the Church," she said, rising to her feet. "He is not to be harmed."

"He's turned her mind," Thomas spluttered, growing red in the face. "Luis, you promised I should have her."

"And so you shall," Don Luis answered. He looked at his daughter and was aware of the open defiance in her expression. Maria Elena had gained courage from somewhere, he would have to be careful how he handled her.

"Listen to me, *niña*, it is time you knew what is going on around you. King Philip has a fine armada gathering at Cadiz. Soon it will sail for England and when it reaches the Channel, our people will rise up and burn the ships anchored in the harbours. Elizabeth and her Protestant brood will be helpless. Reinforcements will come from the Netherlands to aid us, no – to ensure a victory. The King will richly reward those who are loyal. Think, my daughter, you will be able to ask for anything you want. Will you betray your own flesh and blood for a man who has only hate in his heart for us all and who has used you despicably?"

"I will not betray you, Father, nor will I stand by while you murder my husband. I want no part of your schemes. May I have your leave to go?"

Manuel started forward, only to be restrained by Don Luis.

"You are a Choulqueras," he said to his daughter. "When the time comes, you will act like one. Our lives are in your hands."

Thomas Wyndham waited until the door had closed behind Maria Elena and then he turned to Don Luis unbelievingly.

"You let her go? She'll go straight to MacDonald and tell him."

"You underestimate her loyalty to me. The girl believes herself to be in love, any fool can see that, but she won't betray her father."

"I could persuade her to help us. We might even use her to kill MacDonald," Manuel suggested.

"No, my son, I fear you would be over-enthusiastic this time. We must employ more subtle methods, I think we will use MacDonald's mistress to trap him. Sit down, Manuel, you too, Thomas, you both have parts to play in my plan. You are going to be accused of being Maria Elena's lover, Thomas."

"Are you out of your mind?"

"Do not worry, you won't have to fight anyone. I shall hear of this monstrous accusation against my daughter's honour and of course, I shall come to her defence by challenging her accuser."

"But MacDonald won't believe such a fantastic story," Manuel breathed.

"Yes he will, my son, when my trap is spring he will have to believe the evidence of his own eyes. You will see. Be patient."

The repairs to the *Nemesis* took, not one day but three, and Adam slept on board instead of going home. He returned to the house on the afternoon of the third day with thoughts of Maria Elena uppermost in his mind. He had been finding it difficult to concentrate on anything else during his absence. His attitude towards her was a constant source of worry, and he did not know why. He had dealt with her far less harshly than she deserved.

He bathed and changed into fresh clothes and went down to his study, where he immediately poured himself a drink – and then another. Soon he was drinking steadily, without noticing the amount or enjoying it.

"Shall I lay the small table for ye in here or will ye eat in the dining-room?"

Jamie stood in the doorway, regarding him with a disapproving frown. He had put a fresh decanter of whisky on the tray only an hour before and now it was almost empty.

"In here, it's warmer," Adam answered.

"If ye go on drinking ye'll not feel the cold or anything else," Jamie said sourly. "It's her upstairs, isn't it?"

"Mind your own damned business."

"Ye can be as rude as ye like, I'm used to it. I've cared for ye since ye were a bairn. I know every look – every black mood. It's her all right. If ye want her that much, who not go to her?"

Adam swore under his breath.

"Damn your interfering old soul. I'll see her in hell before I do that."

"Aye, no doubt you will," Jamie said and turned to go.

"Wait. Have two places laid in the dining room and ask my wife to join me. Well, don't stand there grinning, man." Adam laughed. He would not go to Maria Elena, but it would not be a weakening of his resolutions if she came to him.

When Jamie returned, he looked more miserable than before.

"The mistress begs to be excused. She has a headache and is retiring early."

Adam went white with anger. Every time he attempted a kind gesture, she flung it back in his face. Let the Spanish bitch stay in her room, what did he care? His temper quickened by raw liquor, he hurled his glass against the nearest wall and stalked out of the house.

Caroline was still with the Queen when he arrived in her rooms. He had her maid bring him a bottle of wine and then dismissed her. Contrary to the gossip linking him with Caroline, he had not seen her for two weeks. She had accepted his marriage to Don Luis' daughter with nothing more than a few subtle remarks and had laughed with him over the taking of the *Santa Margarita*, as she tried on the sapphire bracelet he had brought her – part of the plunder from the sunken ship. They made love as usual, but it left Adam cold and as the days passed he found himself withdrawing further from her. He frequented the Duchess's tavern a great deal, staying there until dawn sometimes in the company of his crew and at times, with the Duchess herself.

She puzzled him. Often she was the coarse, vulgar

whore he expected to find in such an establishment, but there were occasions when they had sat and talked for hours and he had discovered another side to her nature. Once when he had been more than a little drunk, she had begun talking of her ill-fated marriage and her voice had taken on a new tone quite unlike any he had heard her use before, and he realised that she had been born into a world far different to the one she now lived in. Women, he thought digustedly, none of them could be taken at face value.

Caroline arrived an hour after his arrival and found him sprawled on her bed, his arms folded beneath his head.

"Adam, you're early."

"I came to take you out to dinner. I'm bored with my own company."

"Didn't you receive my note? I sent it by a special messenger. I thought we could dine here, everything is arranged." She bent over him and took the bottle from his side. "You've had enough of this."

Adam sat up. The muzziness in his head did not improve the depressive mood he had lapsed into while waiting for her.

"Don't fuss," he snapped.

"I'm sorry. Shall we eat now, or later?"

"What's to prevent us eating now?" he said ungraciously.

Caroline did not retaliate. She had seen this mood before and knew it would be unwise to show her displeasure. Besides, tonight it did not matter how miserable he was as long as she could detain him until midmight. Luis Choulqueras was paying her well to ensure she did.

Adam became more cheerful as the evening progressed, and Caroline allowed herself to relax and enjoy his company. He would never suspect the part she had played in his wife's downfall and he would turn to her for solace as in the past. Nothing, no one was going to take him from her, certainly not a little upstart Spanish girl.

"What are you smiling at?" Adam demanded from the far side of the table.

"Was I smiling? No reason, I'm just happy," Caroline said softly. She rose from her chair and stretched out her hand. "Come and sit on the couch with me."

Her eyes fell on the tiny ornate clock on the buffet as they sat down. Nine o'clock. Thomas Wyndham would be collecting the Choulqueras girl at this moment. The stupid little fool would go with him like a lamb to the slaughter. Don Luis had thought of everything.

Not for a moment did she doubt the story he had told her. Playing the anxious father to perfection, he told her that he was seeking to free his daughter from a loveless marriage and to do so, needed Caroline's help. She believed every word and was willing to do anything to have Adam to herself again. An annulment was out of the question, Don Luis explained; MacDonald had refused to discuss it and therefore it had been necessary to devise more drastic measures to separate him from his beloved daughter. His plan was foolproof provided everyone did their part, he assured her and after its success, Adam MacDonald would be glad to be rid of his wife.

Caroline's part was the simplest of all. She was to arrange a rendezvous with Adam and keep him by her side until after twelve, when she would casually let slip a dangerous piece of gossip.

Only another three hours and then he would be hers again. She lay close against him, promising herself that she would make him forget the other woman. The thought of him holding his wife had given her many a sleepless night.

"Adam." She looked up into his half-closed eyes. "You're almost asleep."

"No, comfortable. Where are you going?"

"To undress."

He watched her begin to unfasten her gown. Although she knew he was watching her, she showed no signs of embarrassment and he frowned, comparing her to the frightened girl who had stood before him on their wedding night, blushing to the roots of her hair. Damn her, he thought savagely. She was becoming a thorn in his side. He rose quickly from the couch, remarkably steady for a man who had consumed so much liquor, and lifted his mistress on to the bed.

After they had made love, she fell asleep contentedly holding on to his arm, while Adam lay restlessly in the darkness, wondering how to tell her he would not be visiting her again.

"Are you sure my father is to meet us here?" Maria Elena asked.

"Of course, my dear, why else should we be here? Try a little of this wine, it's excellent," Thomas Wyndham said, filling her glass to the brim and then the one in front of him.

Maria Elena hesitated, but she was cold and the wine might help to warm her. What in the world had possessed her father to send Sir Thomas to fetch her at nine o'clock at night, and bring her to a rowdy tavern by the docks? They had arrived in a closed carriage and entered by a side door leading directly to the tavern. She had been forced to thrust her way through drunken, jostling men and their crude remarks to the upstairs room where she now sat. It was vaguely reminiscent of the one Adam had brought her to, but as she had no way of knowing where she had been brought, she decided most tavern rooms would look the same. Her curiosity at length drew her to the window, but it was too dark to see if the *Nemesis* was anchored across the water.

"What is this place called?"

"Hades – a stupid name," Thomas answered, trying not to sound as if he knew it too well. "Why?"

"My husband brought me here once. I find it hard to understand why my father has arranged to meet us in the very place where he might encounter the man he hates so much."

Thomas' pale eyes dwelt on her face for a moment. What a waste of time this was, but he had to wait for the drugged wine to take effect.

"You know your husband is otherwise occupied with a certain lady of the Queen's household."

"My father could have come to the house himself," Maria Elena said coldly. She reached for her glass, only to find it empty. Thomas immediately refilled it, his face wreathed in smiles. She had noticed nothing amiss – good.

"Don Luis is a careful man, my dear. He would risk neither an unexpected encounter with your husband, nor the chance of servants gossiping that you had entertained a visitor while alone in the house. You said yourself, young MacDonald knows of the way you tried to deceive him. God knows what mischief he would suspect if you saw your father in his absence."

Maria Elena nodded. When he explained it like that there seemed to be no harm in being in the tavern.

"Why does my father wish to see me?"

"A messenger from King Philip is to disembark from an incoming ship within the hour. He has news of the utmost importance. You see how your father still thinks of you as one of us? You should be grateful to him."

Maria Elena would rather have been in her warm bed, but she did not say so. As time passed she began to feel drowsy and exceedingly warm. Even after removing her cloak, the drowsiness still persisted.

"Are you tired, my dear?"

Thomas leaned across the table and his hand covered hers. His breath was close enough for her to feel his hot breath on her cheek and she drew back in revulsion.

"Yes, I am. Isn't my father late?"

"Perhaps he's been detained in the palace, but I suspect he's taking a roundabout route to prevent anyone following him," Thomas said smoothly.

His face was reddened by drink and he was beginning to grow bolder. He watched her take another sip of her drink, contemplating what she would be like in bed. Despite her protest, he filled her glass again, and swore as he spilled some on to the table.

"Damn, this bottle's empty."

He staggered to the door and flinging it open, bellowed for someone to bring another bottle. Maria Elena stretched an unsteady hand towards her glass and quickly withdrew it. No – it was having the strangest effect on her. Her limbs were growing heavy, making it an effort to move; to think.

" 'Ere we are then." Bessie came through the door, allowing it to slam noisily after her and put down two fresh bottles of wine on to the table. She grinned cheekily at Sir Thomas and received a playful slap on her behind. As she looked at the woman, recognition dawned.

"Guess who's upstairs?" On her way back to the kitchens, she paused at the table where the Duchess sat with a customer. "Sir Thomas and his fancy piece."

"How many times have you been told no names," the Duchess snapped.

"You didn't see what I did. It's 'er that was with Captain MacDonald. You know, the foreign one."

"You're seeing things. Get back to your customers," the Duchess ordered, but the moment Bessie had gone, the woman rose to her feet. "I'll be back in a minute, dearie."

She did not believe for one moment that Bessie was right, not until she opened the door and saw her.

"What the devil do you want?" Thomas spluttered. He was standing behind Maria Elena's chair, watching her and smiling in satisfaction as the drug he had administered to the first bottle of wine, continued to sap her strength.

"I knocked, my lord, did you not hear me? I fear that fool girl has brought you inferior wine." The Duchess picked up one of the bottles, pretending to examine it, while in fact she was studying Maria Elena. *Good God, she's drunk*, Sarah MacDonald thought – *or drugged*. There was a pallor about her cheeks that was not quite right.

Maria Elena raised her head as if only then aware of her presence. Her eyes had a dazed look in them, and she did not recognise the woman who stood before her.

"Is my father coming?"

"Soon, soon, my dear," Thomas murmured.

"I don't want to wait any longer. I am too tired." Maria Elena tried to rise, but her legs refused their support and she sank back into the chair. "Please send for the carriage."

Sarah looked at Thomas Wyndham and knew she had guessed right.

"Shall I bring fresh wine, my lord, or will you not be needing it now?"

Thomas caught her by the arm and hurried her to the door. He pressed a fistful of coins into her hand.

"The lady and I don't want to be disturbed. Do you understand?"

"The lady seems tired."

"A little too much wine, it'll pass. No one is to come up here. Give me any trouble and I'll have this place closed down."

I'll give you trouble, Sarah thought spitefully as she went downstairs. The little fool clearly wasn't willing, then why had she come with him and how had she got out of Adam's tender care? *Adam!* Thought of him halted her in her tracks. She harboured no maternal thoughts towards Maria Elena, but the girl was her son's wife. Let him deal with them both.

She stopped at a table where three sailors sat and dismissed the girls with them.

"Bob, Harry, stay close to the stairs. There's a couple in the first room and I want them kept there at all costs.

There's free ale for you afterwards." She drew the third man aside and spoke to him in low undertones for several minutes before rejoining the customer she had been sitting with earlier.

CHAPTER SEVEN

"FINISH your drink, my dear," Thomas said and moved it closer to Maria Elena's hand.

"I do not want it. Please, take me home, Sir Thomas. If my husband discovers my absence, he will be worried."

Worried, Maria Elena thought. No, not that – suspicious, and she did not want another argument. How unbearably hot the room had become. Her head was aching madly. She would go home and let her father contact her there. She became aware of Thomas Wyndham standing beside the chair, so close that his leg touched hers. He held out a glass before her swimming vision.

"Finish your wine, my beautiful one."

The caress in his tone alarmed her and she stood up quickly. The room spun in circles around her and she put out her hands for support and found herself in his arms. His lips wandered over her hair, her face, down to the white throat and then back to her mouth to subject her to savage, burning kisses. The terror which seized Maria Elena momentarily gave strength to her weakened limbs and she fought him for a few desperate moments before collapsing in tears in his grasp.

"You see how hopeless it is, my dear. Tonight you'll belong to me as you should have months ago," Thomas sneered.

She turned her face away, but he caught her chin and forced her to look up at him. He could see her trying to fight off the slow, relentless immobilising of her brain, but the nearness of his victory was mirrored by the terrible fear in her eyes.

"You are – mad. My father – will – kill you."

To her horror he began to chuckle. It was the most spine-chilling sound she had ever heard and she knew she was lost.

"Who do you think devised this little scheme? I told him that unless I had you, I'd withdraw my support from his precious cause."

"And afterwards?" Maria Elena gasped. She could not believe he was serious. "My husband will kill you."

"Don Luis has plans for him too. You will be a widow within a week."

The whole vile plan was suddenly clear to Maria Elena. With the last of her strength she hit him in the face and broke free, backing away until the hard edge of the bed touched her legs.

"You are a fighter," Thomas declared. "Most people would be unable to think clearly by now. Don Luis said the drug was slow, but he, too, underestimated your spirit." He pulled a chair between the bed and the door and sat down, after ensuring he was within easy reach of the wine bottles. "I'll sit here and enjoy the wine until you become completely insensible. Do your legs feel weak yet? In a moment they won't support you at all. Be sensible and lie down before you fall."

He saw Maria Elena's eyes dart towards the door.

"Who will hear you scream with the rabble below? And I made sure we won't be disturbed. With so much at stake, nothing has been left to chance."

Maria Elena clutched at the heavy curtains to keep her balance. This had to be a nightmare. Then as she felt a numbing coldness stealing through every part of her body, she knew it was a nightmare, but not one from which she would awake and find herself safely at home in the sanctuary of her own bed.

"Why?" Her voice was so weak it was hardly audible.

"I want you more than any other woman I've ever known. I'll teach you to love me, Maria Elena. It may take time, but in the end you'll accept me. After tonight, you'll have no other choice."

Slowly Maria Elena lowered herself down on to the bed. No strength now remained in her body, but she was still able to think comparatively clearly. If she kept on talking, perhaps she could fight off the drug. As long as she did not lose consciousness. . . .

"I will never love you. I hate and despise you. I am in love with Adam MacDonald."

"That is of little consequence." Thomas took a long drink and belched loudly. His manners were atrocious when he was sober, drunk he was coarser than the lowest seaman. "You are a great disappointment to us all, Maria Elena."

"Nothing can change the way I feel."

"MacDonald will do that when he discovers our meeting here," Thomas said. His voice was slurring and the words hardly recognisable. "I've told you nothing has been left to chance, even his mistress is helping us. At this moment he is with her, holding her in his arms. Do you hear me — in his arms? Making love to a cheap whore instead of his wife. She'll tell him about us and he'll come here and find you unconscious on the bed. He'll think you're drunk."

He rose from his chair and started towards her, stretching out thick, clumsy hands to grasp her arm. The plan had been to wait until she was insensible and then leave her lying in bed, partially clothed, but the long hours of waiting and the heavy wine had inflamed his desire to the point where only the final act could satisfy him.

Adam had made up his mind. He would not visit Caroline again. He got out of bed and began to dress quickly, hoping to leave while she slept, but as he was fastening his shoulder cape she opened her eyes and looked across to where he stood.

"Darling, why are you dressed? What time is it?"

"Almost eleven."

Alarm flashed into her eyes and she sat up, hurriedly pulling on a wrap. Why had he chosen tonight of all nights to leave her so early?

"Where are you going?"

"Home."

Less than ten minutes away. Damn him, Caroline thought furiously as she slipped out of bed, his contradictory moods could ruin everything.

"Adam, has this evening bored you?"

She never knew what prompted her to ask the question. Perhaps it was became they had been happy before they went to bed, and now he was anxious to leave while she slept.

"Bored? No, I doubt if any man will ever be bored in your company."

"Then why are you leaving at this hour?"

"I'm not your husband," Adam snapped. "I come and go as I please."

"No, you are hers. Are you going to her now?"

"If I wish." Adam's eyes hardened angrily at what he believed to be a deliberate attempt to provoke an argument. He was not going to Maria Elena, but if Caroline believed otherwise, it could be the reason to end their association.

Sometimes at night after returning from the tavern he was tempted to go to his wife's room, and one night had actually sat in the darkness of her sitting-room for over an hour before going to bed without disturbing her. She had tried to deceive him. She had made him want to trust her, and for that he could never forgive her.

"And if it pleases you I suppose you'll come back here tomorrow and expect me to go to bed with you," Caroline said shrilly.

"No," Adam said, "I won't be coming back again. It's over between us."

She looked stunned, as if he had struck her. He was

joking. But then she looked into his eyes and knew she had already lost him.

"You're leaving me – for her?" she said unbelievingly.

"My wife has nothing to do with it." Even as he spoke, Adam knew it was a lie. She had everything to do with it.

"You fool! You blind, arrogant fool. Go to her, then, see if I care. You'll soon come crawling back to me."

"You know me better than that," Adam scathed. "You won't be troubled with my presence again."

Humiliation swept over Caroline and in its wake came unsurpassed hatred, goading her on to recklessness she was later to regret.

"Nor you with hers." She spat the words at him, her face a mask of hate. "When you are here with me, you don't think she's at home pining for her husband, do you?"

Adam stiffened and turned in the doorway and she saw he had grown considerably paler.

"My wife knows better than to displease me."

"Perhaps her lover has given her confidence," Caroline sneered. She no longer cared about Luis Choulqueras or his precious plan as long as she prevented Adam from giving her up.

"Lover?" Adam repeated quietly. She knew his soft tone to be an indication of great anger.

"Yes, the man you stole her from, Sir Thomas Wyndham."

"That fat pig! My dear Caroline, she loathes the man. Had you named any other, I might have believed you, but him – never."

Unless she acted quickly, he would leave her, Caroline realised. What did it matter if Thomas was still at the tavern; his presence would be the proof Adam needed.

"Very well." She sat down on the stool beside the bed and smiled at him. "Go, if you must and I'll give you a parting gift — proof of your wife's unfaithfulness. Whenever we are together, she sups with Sir Thomas at a tavern in Wapping, called Hades."

"Don't try my patience too far. She'd hardly use a tavern she knows I frequent."

"I didn't know you used the upstairs rooms." She shrugged. "Go and see for yourself, or are you afraid. . . ."

The slam of the door drowned her words. Caroline looked at the clock. Another hour before Adam should have left. In his present mood, if he found his wife with her supposed lover, he might kill them both and that would save everyone a lot of trouble. She climbed back into bed with a satisfied smile. One way and another it had been a most interesting evening.

Adam rode his horse mercilessly through the cobbled streets, driven by a ruthless force he did not understand. By the time he reached the small hamlet of Wapping, he had convinced himself that it was anger he felt because of the disgrace of his wife's indiscrete behaviour would bring on his name. Anger and bitterness — and jealousy.

The Duchess was beside him as he pushed his way to the stairs. She laid a jewelled hand on his arm, but he shook it off. She saw murder in his eyes.

"Where is she?"

"The room at the end of the corridor. I was afraid my messenger wouldn't find you in time."

"I've had no message from you," Adam said roughly. He swept her to one side so violently that only Paco, coming up behind her, saved her from falling. He had been about to leave to go to Ninetta when Adam had stormed past him without seeing him.

"He's crazy, he'll kill them both," Sarah gasped.

"*Si*, I think that is what he means to do."

Adam had reached the end of the passage. Without hesitating he kicked open the door.

Maria Elena could hear loud angry voices somewhere over her head. She neither understood what was being said, nor cared; she wanted to sleep. Someone shook her roughly by the shoulders. She moaned and opened her eyes, but closed them again almost immediately, and began to drift back into unconsciousness.

"Wake up, damn you." She was shaken again, more fiercely than before. Her dulled senses recognised pain and she cried out and opened her eyes on to Adam's glowering features.

"So you're coming out of your drunken stupor at last." He dropped her back on to the bed and stood up.

"I've told you, she's drugged," a woman's voice said close to Maria Elena's ear. She turned and looked into the painted face beside her without recognising it. "You see," the Duchess snapped, "she doesn't know me." She held a glass to Maria Elena's lips, and smiled encouragingly. "Drink a little brandy, there's a good girl."

Maria Elena obeyed, coughing violently as the raw spirits stung her throat. She tried to speak, but her voice was as non-existent as most of her other faculties. She struggled weakly to sit up, and with the Duchess's help at last managed it. And then she saw Thomas Wyndham.

He was sprawled in a heap against the far wall, pinned to the woodwork by a dagger protruding from his left arm. Blood was soaking the sleeve of his jacket and running in narrow rivulets down through his fingers to disappear through the large cracks in the floor. If he was alive or dead she did not know and cared less. The sight of his bloated features revived the terrible nightmare of the last moments before she had fainted. She knew now where she was, and why Adam stood before her with murder written clearly on his face for all to see.

"He – he tricked – me." At last her voice returned; a husky whisper, barely audible. "He said – my – father would – be here. Oh, Adam, thank God you came."

Overcome with relief, she began to cry. It was exactly

what he had expected her to do, and his heart hardened towards her.

"I'm not interested in your lies." His eyes wandered insultingly over his dishevelled form, lingering on the gaping bodice of her gown. "He must have paid you well."

"You can't believe that!"

"If the evidence of my own eyes wasn't enough, Wyndham talked a great deal before I shut him up."

"He lied. . . ."

"You're nearer to death than you've ever been in your life," Adam answered bleakly. "Don't be foolish enough to provoke me further. You're Wyndham's mistress, you have been since we returned to London. At least you might have found yourself a man."

He stared down at the man at his feet who had recovered consciousness and was begging Paco to release him. He would kill him first, Adam decided, and then he would deal with his wife.

"It was her fault. She came to me, pleaded with me to take her from you," Thomas whined. "For God's sake, pull out this dagger, I'm bleeding to death."

Adam bent down and jerked the weapon free and wiped it on Wyndham's breeches. Slowly he turned to look at Maria Elena, the dagger balanced lightly between his fingers.

"Are you going to kill me?" she whispered.

"Why not? You're a liar and a cheat and now you've dishonoured my name. No woman ever betrays a MacDonald – twice."

The Duchess was suddenly between them, blocking his aim.

"You fool, I didn't send for you to come and kill the girl! His precious lordship tampered with the drinks, any idiot can see that. If you don't believe me, take a sniff at one of those bottles."

"Get out of my way, this is none of your business," Adam said between his teeth.

"If you touch me, I'll have half a dozen of my bully boys up here to work you over, Capt'n, and then you'll be in no condition to lay hands on your wife or anyone else," the Duchess warned as Adam's hand bunched into a tight fist. She pointed at Thomas. "It's him you should be threatening."

When Adam still did not move, she swore at him and grabbed one of the bottles of wine. "This is the one they were drinking from when they first arrived. Smell it, damn you, now taste it."

She thrust the bottle into his hand and stood back, hands on her hips. Adam put the neck to his lips and tipped back his head. At first the wine tasted sweet, but as it reached his throat it became bitter and he spat it out. He had been tasting the dregs that Thomas had not bothered to give to Maria Elena, and the presence of something other than wine was only too obvious. Thomas cried out as the bottle smashed into the wall above his head, showering him with broken glass.

"There is a nice deep cellar under the pit," Sarah said meaningly. "No one will hear him screaming."

"Have a couple of your men take him down," Adam replied. He was not looking at her as he spoke, but at his wife. "Tell me the truth. I'll get it out of him anyway."

"You know the wine was drugged, yet you still believe I took a lover," Maria Elena said wearily. "You will not believe anything I say. You want me to crawl on my knees and beg for my life, but I shall disappoint you. Kill me, what do I care? I shall be free of a husband and a family who all hate me." She pulled herself upright by the drapes at the bedside. She was a ghastly colour and near to fainting again. "I have nothing more to say to you."

"Do the MacDonalds kill innocent women?" the Duchess demanded scornfully.

Adam ignored her and beckoned to Paco.

"Take my wife home; lock the door of her room and

see no one goes near her until I return, not even her maid."

"*Si, capitano.*"

Paco picked up Maria Elena's cloak and slipped it around her shoulders. Her pitiful condition aroused his sympathy, but he dared not show it in Adam's company. Adam stepped back to allow them to pass and his eyes ruthlessly searched his wife's ashen face.

"If Wyndham tells me you are his mistress, I'll kill you," he warned.

The cellar beneath the bear-baiting pit ran out under the river. The wooden floor was rotten with damp and water dripped from the walls. Panic-stricken rats scurried away to their holes as Adam followed the Duchess down a flight of stairs to where Thomas Wyndham stood, held in the grasp of two burly sailors. Behind them he saw a massive door, heavily barred, with packing cases stood against it.

"Where does that lead to?" he asked.

"The beach. It used to be an old smuggling route. This whole place is underwater at high tide, very useful for disposing of unwanted items," Sarah said, staring contemptuously at the prisoner. She motioned the two men to release him and go back upstairs. She took a sword from one of them as they passed.

"Well, what are you waiting for?" She turned on Adam impatiently once they were alone. "Make the miserable cur tell you the truth. Unless, of course, you prefer to believe his lies and use them as an excuse to be rid of your wife."

"I don't need excuses, any more than I need you here."

"I've seen men die before."

"You wouldn't dare kill me," Thomas said with a forced show of bravery. In a very short space of time he had become cold sober.

"I can't allow my wife's lover to live," Adam returned.

"You can't kill both of us."

Adam deliberated on the statement for a moment and then said, "Your death should be sufficient to warn her against taking another lover."

Thomas looked into the dark, bleak eyes and then at the fingers curling around the hilt of a sword. He was not a coward, nor was he a fool. Why should he remain silent and die because Luis Choulqueras' plans had not succeeded?

"The truth in exchange for my life?" he said.

"Tell me and you'll be at liberty to walk past me out of here. Lie and I'll cut you down where you stand."

"Your wife came here to wait for her father, at least that's what I told her. It was the Don's idea."

"Why should he ruin his own daughter's reputation?" Adam questioned.

"As her husband you should know that better than anyone. The girl's in love with you. She told Don Luis so and refused to have anything more to do with his schemes."

"Your tongue is too glib, my friend. Even married to me, Maria Elena is still valuable to her father. Perhaps it's not his daughter he wants to be rid of, but you. He knows me well enough to rely on my killing any man who touched a woman of mine."

"It wasn't meant to happen like this, you came too early," Thomas muttered. "That stupid whore you go to was supposed to amuse you until midnight."

Caroline! Adam mouthed the name in silence. Now he understood her strange attitude, and at last accepted that Maria Elena was innocent of the heinous crimes of which he accused her. A pawn she was indeed; first of her father, then his own. The sight of Wyndham bending over her on the bed flashed through his mind. From the doorway as he entered he could see she was making no attempt to break free and he had been incensed with rage. Had Paco not hung on to his sword arm, he would have run them both through. It was obvious now why she had not been struggling, and why she had not attempted to defend herself against his anger.

Alarmed by his silence, Thomas was blurting out the whole sordid story and clutching at his arm as if in his death throes. The Duchess's lips curled in disgust as she watched him.

"Why not let my men unbar the door?" she suggested. "The tide would take him out into the middle of the river, and with his weight he'd sink into the mud like a stone."

Thomas's eyes widened with fear as Adam smiled.

"You promised. I've told you the truth, now let me go."

"I said you'd be free to go past me," Adam said quietly. He drew his sword, stretching out his free hand for the one Sarah was holding. She gave it to him without a word and watched him toss it at the other man's feet.

"This is the second time you've laid hands on Maria Elena against her will. Do you remember the first, in the garden at St. James's, Wyndham? She ran from you then and so you thought to take her tonight when she was drugged and helpless. You've never acted like a man in your life, at least try to die like one. Come past me if you can."

Sarah MacDonald stood on the steps watching the fight which ensued, her eyes intent on Adam's smiling features. He would kill Wyndham, of that she was sure. When it was over, she came down to where he stood and stared at the lifeless corpse at his feet without a trace of emotion on her face.

"You're hurt," she said, looking at the blood on Adam's shirt. "Come upstairs and let me dress the wound."

"My God, you're a cool one!"

Ignoring the contempt in his voice, she climbed the stairs to the upper rooms, locking the door of the cellar behind them and led him to her room at the top of the house. She furnished him with a bottle of whisky while she washed and bandaged the gash in his side.

"I can see you heal well by these other scars on your back. Did you get them all fighting Spaniards?"

"Mostly." Adam stared at her curiously as she took the bottle from him and drank thirstily. "I don't understand your concern for me – or my wife. Why did you try to warn me?"

Sarah laughed softly. She had been waiting for that question all evening. She saw a frown crease his forehead as he looked at her and quickly drew back into the shadows. She had no fears of him recognising her with her disfigured skin and the heavy powder and rouge, but it was as well not to tempt fate. Adam was not soft like his father, he would kill her as surely as Michael MacDonald had forgiven her.

"You and I share a common hatred – Luis Choulqueras."

"For what reason?"

"Personal reasons."

"So you were one of his women too," Adam sneered. He stood up, fastening the front of his shirt.

"It offends you to know I was involved with him?"

"It disgusts me."

Sarah did not pursue the subject. She shrugged and had another drink.

"I'm grateful for your help," Adam murmured. "What you were is not my affair. How can I repay you?"

"Let me be present when you slit the Don's throat," Sarah laughed. "This evening has brought the happy event somewhat closer, don't you agree?"

"Hardly. Don Luis won't call me out over Wyndham, he'll try to persuade the Queen it was cold-blooded murder. She'll listen to me when I tell her I have a witness. You will testify for me?"

He saw her stiffen and waited for a refusal, but she nodded.

"Of course. I was thinking of your wife being in love with you. What a stroke of luck! You have complete control over her now, she'll do anything you say."

"I don't think I'm capable of hating her that much," Adam said with a sudden hardening of his expression. "She's been used as a pawn long enough."

He was still inwardly shaken at the appalling scheme to allow Maria Elena to be seduced. It had Manuel's twisted touch about it.

"Oh, come now," Sarah said bemusedly. "She's a Spaniard and his daughter into the bargain. Take a lesson from the Don and use her."

Adam uttered an oath that made her wince.

"For years I watched my father grovel at my mother's feet in the name of love. He forgot he was a man and master, not only of himself, but of her too." Adam's eyes blazed with a fierce light. "No woman will ever do that to me – nor would I subject my wife to years of humiliation merely to satisfy my hatred of her father. I'd kill her first."

Sarah was quiet for a long time, and beneath the powder, her face was ashen. So he still hated her, after ten years. She had begun to hope. . . .

"To hear you talk I'm inclined to think you're in love with the girl."

Adam spun round on her so abruptly that he knocked over the chair on which he had been sitting.

"I avoid love like the plague," he said harshly and strode out of the room.

The fire had gone out in the sitting-room, but Maria Elena did not ring for a servant to come and light it again. She lay on the couch, her aching head supported by cushions, and waited for Adam to return. There was nothing else to do with Paco standing guard outside the door.

She still felt wretchedly sick and dizzy, but had not fainted again. She was wondering if she had enough strength to reach the bedroom and undress when she heard voices outside. The door was unlocked and Adam entered. With a sinking heart she watched him relock it behind him. It seemed conclusive evidence that Sir Thomas had lied and been believed.

Slowly she rose to her feet, her head tilting proudly as Adam moved across the room to stand in front of her.

"Wyndham is dead," he said in a low tone.

"And now it is my turn?"

A flush stole over the bronzed face before her.

"No, I am here to apologise. Before he died he told me the whole truth."

"Then why did you kill him?" she asked breathlessly.

"What I do to you is my affair, but while you are my wife, I'll never allow another man to touch you."

He stepped forward, gripping her by the wrists as her eyes closed and she began to sway unsteadily.

"It's over, Maria Elena, don't be afraid. I believe he tricked you."

She opened her eyes and looked at him and knew.

"He told you I love you." She shrugged. "It does not matter now."

He did not answer, and she took his silence to mean that he would never believe she loved him, nor would he ever trust her. What was her word against hi hate for her family?

"It doesn't matter," she repeated brokenly. "Nothing matters now. You came – before – he. . . ." she broke off with a shudder. "Is your mistress losing her charms that you left her early?" Her secret was out and it left her with no defence, other than scorn.

"Her company no longer appeals to me, we have parted," Adam said. He longed to draw her head against his chest and give her the comfort he knew she needed, but his pride forbade it, the same pig-headed pride which had kept him from her for so long. And there were other more important things to think of. He had to find out how deeply she was involved in her father's schemes. He could see that she was near to collapse and ruthlessly took advantage of her condition. "Wyndham spoke of a rising in favour of Philip of Spain before he died. Tell me about it."

"I cannot," Maria Elena whispered. "My father would kill me."

"You are going to tell me." Adam pulled her against him, staring down into her tortured face. "I mean to know – how I do is up to you."

"Will you beat me too?" The thought made her feel weaker still.

Adam looked startled.

"Who has touched you? Don Luis? Manuel?"

What little colour there was in Maria Elena's cheeks, vanished at her brother's name. Adam gave a savage expletive.

"When was this?"

"Several weeks ago when – when I refused to be nice – to – you and then later, Sir Thomas. Manuel is a past master at inflicting pain without leaving any tell-tale bruises."

"Force – that's all you've known since you came to England," Adam said gently. "From me, your father, brother. Was it this way in Spain too?"

"Sometimes, when Manuel lost his temper." Maria Elena pressed a hand against her throbbing temples. She was swaying with fatigue. "Do not ask me to betray them, Adam, I beg you. I will do anything else you ask, but not that."

"One day soon you will have to choose which side you're on."

"But not now, I am so confused and my head aches terribly."

"That damned drug!" Adam exclaimed. "I should have realised."

Swinging Maria Elena up into his arms, he carried her into the bedroom. She was a dead weight in his grasp, her head lolling limply back against his shoulder, the long dark lashes lying on cheeks lacking of any colour. *God, she looks ill*, Adam thought and he was as responsible as Wyndham for her collapse.

As he set her down on the bed he realised that she was hardly conscious. Her forehead was wet with perspiration and her skin burned with fever.

"I'll fetch Ninetta," he said, fixing the pillows comfortably beneath her head.

"I had Paco send her to bed. She was very upset, and I had no idea what time you would be back. I had to wait and find out if you believed me."

The stricken look on her face stirred the conscience Adam had suppressed for so long. He bent over her and his mouth gently brushed hers.

"I believe you."

The sight of the tears welling down over her cheeks were more than he could stand. With an oath, he gathered her in his arms and pillowed her head against his shoulder, stroking her hair and whispering soft endearments that he had once sworn no woman would ever hear from his lips. His mother had always swayed his father with tears, which in her case and so many others over the years, he had found to be false and meaningless. But this girl was not his beautiful, wanton mother and these tears were not to arouse his sympathy. There was nothing false about Maria Elena, although it had taken him a long time to find it out. There were many qualities about her that he had grown to admire and respect.

Her skin was growing cold and he realised that she was suffering from the after-effects of the drug. She clung to him like a frightened child as he stripped off the torn gown she wore and moved alongside her in the bed, warming her body with his own until the tremulous sobs died away and she lay quiet and still.

Maria Elena raised her head and looked at him, many tears still lingering in the depths of her green eyes. Adam's heart almost stopped beating. Cupping the small, pale face in his hands he pressed his mouth to hers. For a moment there was nothing, then her lips parted beneath his and with her response was awakened in him something he had never believed possible – the knowledge that he was capable of love.

CHAPTER EIGHT

ADAM had just finished breakfast the next morning when Francis Drake arrived, accompanied by half-a-dozen men at arms.

"Francis, come in. Have you eaten yet?"

"This morning I have little stomach for food," Francis Drake said gravely.

Adam's gaze flickered past his unsmiling face to the soldiers who had stationed themselves on each side of the front door and his mouth tightened.

"Come into the study. Am I under arrest?" he asked when they were alone.

"House arrest, yes."

"The Queen has my letter with the particulars of what happened. On what charge am I detained?"

"Murder, boy. The charge is murder."

"Since when has it been murder to kill the man attempting to rape your wife?" Adam demanded angrily. His letter had been brief and to the point. Surely someone had talked to the Duchess and confirmed his story?

Drake took the glass of wine Adam held out to him and stood, ill at ease, beside the window.

"We've been friends for a long time, Adam, let us at least be truthful with each other. This Spanish girl means nothing to you, her honour does not come into it. Through her you wanted to get at Don Luis, that's all."

"No," Adam said firmly, "that's not all." He drank his whisky and replenished the glass before crossing to where his friend stood. "Part of what you say is true, I did marry

Maria Elena to reach her father, and my intention to kill him and his bastard still stands." His fingers lightly traced the scar on his cheek and his eyes burned with hatred. "I swore on my father's grave that I wouldn't rest until they are dead, even if the deed exiles me to the seas for the rest of my life."

"And the girl?"

"She is my wife, she'll come with me. She happens to be in love with me."

"How very fortunate for you," Drake said dryly. "You have a powerful weapon there."

Adam swore savagely and Drake saw he had paled considerably.

"My God, hasn't she been used enough? For love of me she's borne beatings from her brother by refusing to use her position to spy on me. She's been humiliated by me worst of all, and also by the trash that inhabit the court, and then Don Luis hatched last night's little plot to make me believe she'd taken a lover."

"Then the account you gave the Queen was the truth?"

Francis stared at him bleakly, wanting desperately to believe him, yet unable to accept Adam would kill a man over the daughter of his bitterest enemy.

"Yes it was. My word is my bond, old friend. Have you ever known me to lie?"

Drake had to admit he had not.

"Wyndham took Maria Elena from this house on the pretext that she was to meet her father," Adam went on. "At a tavern in Wapping, he gave her drugged wine and then tried to rape her. I was with Caroline – that was not accidental – the Don paid her to keep me occupied, but for reasons I intend keeping to myself, she failed and I came away early. Her parting shot was to tell me where I could find my wife and her supposed lover. I got to Maria Elena in time, thank God. . . ."

"Your letter mentions a woman called the Duchess who runs this tavern."

"We're old drinking friends. For some reason she sent a messenger to warn me what was happening."

"You have a strange ally in that woman," Francis murmured.

"I shall be for ever grateful to her. What happened when I reached the tavern is of no importance, except to Maria Elena and myself. When I had sent her home, Wyndham and I fought and I killed him. It was a fair fight, ask the Duchess."

"She's disappeared. My soldiers searched the place from top to bottom this morning and there's not a sign of her. They found the body of Sir Thomas in the cellar, but apart from that there were only serving wenches there. Needless to say, Don Luis has been with the Queen since early this morning accusing you of a cruel and senseless murder. She had no choice, Adam, she was forced to order you confined to the house, until a witness can be produced to confirm your story." Drake put aside his glass and turned to the door. "I'll do what I can to find the Duchess for you."

"And if you don't?" Adam asked, following him out into the hall.

"I prefer not to think about it. The alternative is to stand trial for murder, and we both know if that happens the Spaniard will see to it you are found guilty."

A startled gasp from behind brought Adam wheeling about, his eyes circling upwards to the landing where Maria Elena stood staring down at them. She had a robe over her petticoats and her black hair streamed loosely past her shoulders to accentuate the terrible pallor of her cheeks. She opened her mouth as if to speak, then began to sway, and before the horrified gaze of the two men below, she slowly crumpled to the ground.

Adam cried out her name and leapt up the stairs two at a time to reach her side and lift her into his arms.

"A doctor, Francis, quickly, she's feverish again."

There was a glitter in his eyes that Drake had never seen

before and he thought he knew all Adam's unpredictable moods. This one was a mixture of gentleness and madness. Was he fond of the girl after all? If he was and anything happened to her, no soldiers on earth would be able to stop him seeking out Luis Choulqueras.

"For God's sake, didn't you hear me?" Adam said hoarsely. "She's ill from that drug Wyndham gave her. If you're worrying about me trying to escape, forget it. Nothing will induce me to leave Maria Elena until I know she's going to be all right – and if she isn't, a thousand men couldn't keep me in this house."

He strode past Drake with his unconscious burden without waiting for an answer and heard him calling loudly for a servant as he entered Maria Elena's bedroom.

"Your Majesty, the woman refuses to go away. She told me to give you this."

Elizabeth looked up angrily at the servant standing before her, but the order to have the mysterious woman who had been asking for an audience thrown out of the palace, died on her lips. The servant held in the palm of his hand a ruby of magnificent size which she immediately recognised.

"This woman. What's her name?"

"She calls herself the Duchess, Your Majesty. It's a nickname the seamen gave her, I believe. She owns the tavern called Hades in Wapping."

The place where Sir Thomas had met his death, the Queen thought. Adam MacDonald's one and only witness in his defence.

"Give me the jewel and bring her in."

Elizabeth sat lost in thought, turning the ruby over and over between her fingers. It was of great significance to her, but how it had come into the possession of a whore was a mystery. If the Duchess was not prepared to say whence it came, a while in the Tower would soon restore her memory, she mused.

The woman who knelt before her was shrouded from head to toe in a coarse cloak. She had even hidden her face. Elizabeth dismissed the servants hovering nearby with an annoyed frown. She hated prying ears.

"Get up and tell me how you came by this ruby. Did you buy it? Steal it?"

"Neither. Your Majesty gave it to me on my wedding day, if you remember," Sarah MacDonald said quietly, and pulled back her hood.

"I am here on my knees to beg Your Majesty for my son's life."

Elizabeth sprang from her chair as if there was a sword point behind her.

"Ten years have changed me, haven't they?" Sarah's voice turned suddenly bitter. "Even Adam doesn't recognise me. I would not have revealed myself to you had he not been arrested."

"Sarah," the Queen said softly. "Sarah Chalmers."

"Then Sarah MacDonald. Now the Duchess – a woman of dubious character, consort of thieves and murderers."

"And with damn' little future if your son finds out you are alive," Elizabeth retorted. "Come, sit here beside me. I want to know the whole sordid story, perhaps I can help."

As children they had been close friends and Elizabeth was not a woman who discarded friends easily – they were too few and far between for a Queen to do that.

"I want nothing for myself. I came for Adam's sake." It was only the second time Sarah had used his name since the day she had stood by and watched Manuel inflict the wound in his cheek. She had watched and done nothing, except call out his name, once, before she turned and ran from the bitterness and hate in her son's face – away from the sight of blood and the husband she had forsaken.

"Captain MacDonald stands accused of murder. There are no witnesses to say it was a fair fight, as he claims," Elizabeth said. "Do you really own this tavern, Hades?"

"Yes. I was also present at the fight. Do you know why Adam came to my tavern in the first place?"

Elizabeth nodded. It was an ugly business and had left an unpleasant taste in her mouth. Surely she had enough problems trying to arrange her cousin's quiet demise without one of her best sea captains getting himself executed for murder? She would be needing him and more like him with Philip of Spain's armies patiently sitting across the Channel in the Netherlands, waiting for her to make a mistake. Mary would have to go – and that meant war.

She sighed and asked Sarah for a full account of the story. She listened in silence, watching the face of the woman who had been her childhood companion, and pitied her.

Ten years before, Michael MacDonald had stood where Sarah now sat and begged leave to be relieved of his duties so that he could follow the wife who had deserted him to flee with another man – one Don Luis Choulqueras. He had spoken of the house in the Highlands which had been put to the torch and of the murder of his servants. Elizabeth had not denied his request, any more than she would deny Sarah's plea for her son. Adam MacDonald's hatred of the Spaniards, and one in particular, had been a great asset to her over the years. In return for his commission as a privateer, he had brought her many richly laden treasure chests and valuable information gained from months in Spanish waters.

It was his sight of the ships gathering at Cadiz which had first warned her of impending attack and confirmed her fears of a Popish plot. The harbours were under constant surveillance, men watched the coastal roads. When Philip's messenger arrived to contact his English spies, she would be waiting and the identities of all those involved would be made known to her.

"Captain MacDonald will be informed that he is no longer under arrest." Elizabeth smiled into Sarah's worried face. "It has been very difficult for you to come here, but I'm glad you did. It was a black day for me when your husband whisked you away to the Highlands and deprived me of the only woman I have ever been able to confide in. Were you happy?"

"I had to betray him before I learned what happiness was," Sarah said, and was shocked to feel hot tears sting her eyes. "I behaved like a whore. Luis Choulqueras made me one. He was unfaithful to me even when I was with him, and after two years he tired of me. He came to the house one day and told me to leave – just as I was. I argued, pleaded with him at least to give me enough money to come back to England. He laughed in my face and gave me to one of his soldiers."

Elizabeth reached out and tugged at the silken cord hanging at her side. The servant who answered the summons was amazed to be told that all audiences were cancelled and no one was to enter the Queen's private apartments for the rest of the day, unless specifically called. The palace servants had much to gossip about that evening.

For a day and a night Maria Elena lay in bed with a raging fever, recognising no one. On the second day her temperature dropped and she fell into a peaceful sleep. Not until this happened did Adam stir from her side to snatch a few hours' rest. He was hardly aware of the armed guards at his door. His own future was suddenly unimportant with Maria Elena lying ill, and he gave no thought to his predicament at all during the long hours he kept a constant vigil beside her bed.

Jamie came to him early on the third morning to say that the soldiers had withdrawn. Before Adam had recovered from his surprise a messenger brought a letter from the Queen, written in her own hand. In it she said that a witness had come forward and completely cleared him of the murder charge, and she now believed that he had acted in defence of his wife's honour. There was also an invitation to dine with her later in the month.

The witness was not named, but Adam knew it could only be the Duchess. Jamie smiled when he heard the news and said that heaven had heard his prayers. He was surprised at Sarah's intervention, but grateful. It was a pity Adam must never know he owed his life to his mother.

Adam was beside Maria Elena when the last of the fever left her, and she opened her eyes for the first time in three long days. Memory came flooding back and with it fears for the safety of the man she loved.

"Adam, the soldiers." She started up in alarm, struggling against the restraining hands he laid on her shoulders. "I must go to the Queen and tell her the truth."

"Gently, little one. I'm no longer under arrest."

She sank back on to the pillows bewildered.

"But – this morning. . . ."

"The day before yesterday," Adam corrected. "You've been ill." Making her more comfortable, he explained in quiet, unhurried tones about the Queen's letter.

"I am glad," Maria Elena whispered.

Adam frowned down at her.

"Then why did you keep your feelings secret from me for so long? Were you afraid I'd throw them back in your face?"

"Yes – and you would have. You called me a liar and a cheat; I tried to be both to please my father – and failed." Her voice faltered and he saw huge tears glistening in her eyes. "I don't deserve the awful things you said about me. I do love you. I can tell you now because I know my father has no more use for me and therefore my usefulness to you is also finished. Do with me what you will, my husband. I am at your mercy – as always."

Her words jarred Adam. She was vulnerable as she had never been before. Too weak to retaliate to his baiting remarks or to bear his scorn, or to refuse him if he made love to her. He turned away and walked to the window. It was snowing outside and the Thames was almost frozen over, trapping the *Nemesis*. He could not up anchor and sail away from the responsibility of what he had helped to do. In his own way he was as guilty as Thomas Wyndham and Luis Choulqueras.

Do with me what you will. Submission to her fate no matter what he proposed. He could not hurt her – the old anger was no longer in him. He looked at her lying in the huge bed, the long black hair spread out on each side of her pale face like a dark cloud, and realised that he too had become vulnerable.

"Doesn't it hurt to know I don't care for you?" he asked, in a rougher tone than he intended.

Slowly Maria Elena shook her head.

"You forget I have been raised for a marriage without love. I am happy you did not laugh at me – and grateful."

"Why should I laugh?"

A faint flush of colour stole into her cheeks as he moved, frowning, to the end of the bed.

"I – I know I am not like your other women," she stammered.

"A fact I found pleasing, despite what I said to the contrary. Experienced women are a bore."

Maria Elena was silent. She had never seen him in this strange mood before.

"It's time you forgot your Spanish training and became a woman," Adam said quietly. "You are a woman, Maria Elena, make no mistake about that, although your father and brother have done their best to make you feel a chattel. Submission and obedience could be far pleasanter mixed with response. You might even discover that I'm not the inhuman monster you believe me to be."

"I was a weapon to be used to further your revenge," Maria Elena said, a break in her voice. "Because of my love I will never refuse you, or betray you in any way, not even to my own family, but I can never forget my position here."

Adam straightened, his face unreadable.

"I've never lied to you. When we were first married, I fully intended to use you in whatever way I could – that's no longer the way of it." He paused beside the door and looked back at the surprised look on her wan features. "Your position here is as my wife. I suggest you consider it most seriously," he added softly, and left her alone.

At the end of the week the doctor pronounced Maria Elena well enough to get up. Less than an hour after Ninetta had dressed her in a warm gown and installed her on the couch in the sitting-room, Adam came into the room. Maria Elena had ceased to be surprised at his unexpected visits. he came to see her every day and ask how she was. His change of attitude brought her great happiness.

"The Queen has gone to Hampton Court. She invited us to join her there, but I explained that you were not strong enough yet."

"Of course." Disappointment showed in her eyes before she looked away. It was too much to hope that he would publicly acknowledge the new relationship between them.

"I did assure her, however, that we wouldn't miss the pageant on Friday evening. As long as you don't dance yourself into the ground, a few hours away from the house will do no harm."

"Oh, Adam, are we going?"

Her face broke into an excited smile and he felt as if the room was suddenly flooded with sunshine. He laughed softly, pleased at her response. It would do no harm, as he said and it would show Luis Choulqueras that he had lost an ally. Caroline would be there, and the opportunity would perhaps arise to repay her for her treachery. He had not visited her again, nor had he replied to the many messages she had sent. She was part of his life he was wishing did not exist.

After long deliberation Maria Elena decided that she would have a new gown made for the occasion. She chose white brocade, which had traced on it a delicate design in silver thread, and deep blue velvet to be made into a cloak. This was to be trimmed with white ermine to match the gown. She was pleased with her purchases, almost as pleased as the seamstress when her customer chose the most expensive materials she possessed.

Maria Elena's excitement grew as Friday approached and Ninetta found it almost impossible to make her rest. She sorted through her jewel-caskets time and time again, unable to decide what would look best with her gown.

The finished article was exquisite. Styled after the Spanish fashion at Maria Elena's request, it avoided the elaborate puff sleeves and starched ruff so predominant among the court ladies. It was cut low across her breasts with whaleboning skilfully sewn into the bodice, thus dispensing with the necessity of wearing tight-fitting corsets and leaving room for extra petticoats. Ninetta dressed her mistress's hair with extra care that Friday evening, adorning the gleaming coil with a diamond-studded comb and a headdress of white Cordova lace.

Adam came into the room so quietly that neither woman was aware of his presence until he was standing at Maria Elena's side. He dismissed the maid with a wave of his hand, full attention centred on the superbly gowned figure of his wife. She held her breath expectantly. His eyes lingered longest on the sapphires glittering at her throat, then he shook his head.

"Take them off and wear this instead."

From his pocket he drew out a leather case and snapped back the lid. Maria Elena caught her breath at the sight of the magnificent diamonds blazing up at her from the black velvet pad. With trembling fingers she unfastened the sapphire necklace and allowed Adam to fasten the other in its place. Hundreds of tiny stones tapered away from her throat to a diamond of enormous size nestling above her breasts.

"It is a MacDonald heirloom," Adam said. "It's been in my family for generations. By tradition it's yours now."

Maria Elena touched the cold stones against her skin, her eyes puzzled.

"Are you sure you want me to have them? Or is this merely a gesture to flaunt in my father's face when we see him? He will be there, won't he?"

"Yes, but that's not the reason. Say if they offend you and they can go back to the attic again, with the rest of the relics of my heritage."

Maria Elena flushed at his insolent tone and answered, "I am not offended, Adam, but honoured you think me worthy enough to wear them – and very surprised."

"Then don't question my motives again. Are you ready?"

"Yes. May I have my cloak, there, on the bed? Did you really keep this beautiful necklace in the attic?"

"Yes – along with many memories of the past."

"Painful memories?"

He looked down at her questioningly.

"Why do you ask that? You know what lies behind my hatred."

"I know only what you have told me. I think perhaps there is much more. Don't shut me out, please," Maria Elena begged. "Let me love you."

"Be content with things the way they are," Adam snapped. "You are free to come and go as you please without fear of being molested by your father or brother – that alone has made life easier for you. I shall demand your company very little, except on occasions like this when the Queen expects to see us together. The servants have been instructed to take their orders direct from you during my absence, instead of from Jamie. In heaven's name, what else do you want?" His eyes narrowed suddenly and gleamed with derisive mockery. "I may even sleep with you from time to time if you are lonely, but never mention love to me again."

Maria Elena felt angry tears prick her eyes. For a moment she thought she had reached him.

"I was not asking you to come to my bed, but to let me share the memories that have hurt you so deeply. I realise now that it was a stupid hope. I shall not attempt to intrude into your private little world again."

She did not see the look of pain on Adam's face, for he turned quickly away from her, making room for her to pass. With immense dignity she picked up her skirts and made her way downstairs to the waiting carriage.

Elizabeth was in a good humour. She had spent an enjoyable day in the company of friends, hunting despite the bitter cold, and was looking forward to the evening's entertainments. Like her father, Henry VIII, she needed no excuse to give a ball or banquet. Music and good food soothed her frayed nerves and helped her to forget the unfortunate woman under sentence of death in Fotheringay.

The lights from Hampton Court could be seen for miles around. Carriages had been arriving since early afternoon and the downstairs rooms were full of noisy, chattering people. Huge fires blazed in the hearths and were never allowed to die down. It was pleasantly warm everywhere; the atmosphere relaxed and intimate. In the Great Hall hundreds of candles shone their flickering light on the beautiful dresses and breathtaking jewels. Rich carpets and thick tapestries hung around the Hall and long tables had been loaded with refreshments. Full-bodied Malmsey ale, wines from across the channel, sweetmeats and delicacies to tempt any palate.

Maria Elena sat beside Adam at the head of the table nearest the Queen, her face flushed with excitement as she watched a group of mummers performing in the centre of the floor. She could not remember when she had enjoyed herself more.

The performance came to an end and as music came once more from the minstrels' gallery overlooking the Hall, the Queen rose to dance.

Adam rose to his feet, holding out a hand.

"Don't you want to dance?" he asked amusedly as she remained in her seat, dumbfounded.

"Please."

He led her into the midst of the dancers, the smile on his brown face mocking her and completely disguising the way his eyes searched the sea of faces around them. He glimpsed Luis Choulqueras for a moment, standing by his son at the far end of the room. Manuel started forward, but was restrained by his father and they both turned and went outside.

Adam did not mind the jealous looks of other women. He wanted his wife to be the most beautiful woman present, and their envious stares proved that she was. But as the evening progressed he became annoyed by the admiring glances cast her way by other men. Most of them knew him by reputation, if not by name, and tried to conceal their interest; but he noticed them just the same and was angry because he found it impossible to ignore them and remain indifferent.

He began to drink heavily and snapped at Maria Elena when he caught her looking at him in a disapproving fashion.

"May I have the pleasure of dancing with the most attractive woman in the room?"

Francis Drake stood beside their table. He addressed himself to Maria Elena, but his eyes were on Adam, puzzled and a little quizzical as if questioning his lack of attention to the woman at his side.

"Thank you, Captain Drake."

Maria Elena rose quickly to her feet and gave him her hand.

"Adam is a very lucky man," Drake said as they danced. He had been watching her since she arrived and was conscious of many others doing so too. She carried herself well. If she knew of the gossip her appearance had provoked, she did not show it.

"Do you say that because you are his friend, or because you mean it?"

"Why don't you persuade him to take a sea trip? The air would do you both good," Drake murmured, ignoring her question.

"And keep him out of my father's way? I wish I could, Captain Drake, but he will not listen to me. There is a wall between us I cannot break down."

You would not believe that had you seen the look on his face I saw, Drake thought, and wondered if he had been mistaken in his assumption. Adam did not appear to have changed towards her, despite their presence at the dinner.

Maria Elena looked looked across to where Adam sat and her eyes were worried.

"Does he always drink so much?"

"He can hold his liquor. Don't worry, he won't get drunk."

"If he does, my brother will no doubt seize the opportunity to plunge a dagger into his back as we leave," Maria Elena said. She had seen her father and Manuel earlier, but now they had both vanished and she was apprehensive. Their plan to compromise her had failed and not only was one of the chief sources of money and men dead, but she still remained as Adam's wife. Only his immediate death would free her and place her once more in her father's power.

"I don't think so," Drake assured her. "I shall be watching. The Queen sends her condolences over your illness and hopes to see you soon at court."

"Thank Her Majesty for me and say I shall attend her soon. I'm afraid I tire easily, Captain Drake, will you take me back now?"

Adam was on his feet as they returned to the table, staring at someone behind him. Following his gaze, Maria Elena saw a strikingly attractive woman standing in the doorway. Their eyes met and she felt her stomach somersault unsteadily, all her instincts crying out that this was her husband's mistress. One look at his face confirmed it. He turned and saw them and a smile masked his features.

"We are leaving," he said to Maria Elena.

"Good heavens, man, it's not yet twelve," Drake exclaimed. "Besides, I want to dance with your wife again."

"Another time perhaps, my wife is tired, Francis." Adam's tone belied argument. "If you find her company so enjoyable, perhaps you will do me the small favour of escorting her to the carriage. I'll be with you in a few moments."

"Of course," Drake said stiffly. He, too, had seen Caroline Stacey. He ushered Maria Elena out of the room as quickly as possible, hoping she had not realised who the woman was and knowing full well she had.

Maria Elena stopped as they reached the Clock Court and stared up at the ornate chiming clock set in the archway over the path. He could see that she was struggling to compose herself and did not attempt further meaningless conversation. She glanced back in time to see Adam walking towards the red-headed woman.

"Would you mind if I asked you to leave me, Captain Drake?" she said quietly, looking into the sympathetic face beside her.

"If it is what you want." Drake bent and kissed her hand. "Will you be all right?"

"Perfectly. I will admire the gardens until Adam comes."

Drake frowned, but acquiesced. He bade her goodnight and returned to the Great Hall, ignoring the two figures standing close together in the shadowy cloisters.

Caroline had not taken her eyes off Maria Elena the whole evening, and she was consumed with jealousy. The true story of Don Luis' attempt to dishonour his daughter had, of course, come back to her, and she knew that in her desperation to own Adam completely, she had perhaps lost him. She had sent him a note while Maria Elena was dancing, asking him to meet her, but she had not been sure he would accept until he actually stood at her side. His face was in the shadows and she could see neither his expression nor the look in his eyes. Had she been able to, she might not have been so confident of her ability to win him back.

"I was hoping you'd come alone," she said, sending a baleful look after the white blur slowly moving towards the Main Courtyard.

"I thought an evening out would please my wife. She's been ill, as you know,' Adam said stonily.

He too was watching Maria Elena, still amazed by the terrible look of pain he had seen on her face when Caroline appeared.

"When shall I see you again? it's been so long," Caroline whispered.

"It's over. I told you so before."

"My God, you can't mean that." Caroline's voice was harsh with fear. "You – you aren't in love with her?"

Adam made no answer. He did not feel anger, as when Sarah had said almost the same words to him. This time there was a tight knot of pain in his stomach like the slow twisting of a knife.

"You can't love her! I won't let you. Come back to me, Adam, I'll make you forget her. I love you. I only helped Don Luis to have you all to myself. Please – please take me back."

Adam squashed the fierce desire to put his hands around her throat and squeeze the life out of her.

"If we ever meet again alone – no man will want you when I'm through," he said coldly, and strode past her to follow his wife.

CHAPTER NINE

MARIA ELENA was walking down one of the flagged paths which criss-crossed the gardens. Adam quickened his steps to catch up with her, then halted abruptly as a man came out of the trees and stopped in front of her. Light from a torch on the archway above them illuminated his face. Adam swore beneath his breath, and his hand was on his sword as he stepped on to a side path to come around behind them.

"Let me pass, Manuel," Maria Elena said for the second time.

"You and I have to talk first," her brother sneered.

He blocked her way completely. Maria Elena half turned to run, then remembering the two people behind her in the cloisters, she stayed where she was.

"Have you come to apologise? You always were Father's errand boy."

"MacDonald has given you false courage, sister. Hold your tongue, or I'll have to remind you that, married or not, you are still a Choulqueras. Where have you been these past weeks?"

"Ill – thanks to the drug Sir Thomas gave me. How could you surrender me to that man, Manuel? It was a horrible, vile scheme. Thank God Adam came. . . ."

"Adam," Manuel broke in. "Good grief, you're bewitched by the man! It is time you returned to the fold before you are foolish enough to present him with a child."

Maria Elena paled beneath his scorn, but she stood her ground bravely.

"I'm no longer afraid of you, Manuel, or of Father. I see you both for what you are, liars, cheats and whoremongers." She had never before used such language. "Go away and leave me alone."

Manuel's hand snaked out and fastened over her wrist, twisting it cruelly. Her cry of pain brought a smile to his face.

"Father wants to talk to you. He's waiting in our carriage. Our plans are soon to be realised, and he needs you."

Maria Elena began to struggle against his hold, raking at his face with her nails. She suspected that once she was inside her father's carriage, she would never see Adam again. Manuel cursed her in Spanish, slapped her hard across both cheeks and began to drag her after him along the path.

Maria Elena did not see Adam – or the blow he dealt her brother. She suddenly found herself released – and so abruptly that she lost her balance and stumbled. A strong arm went around her waist and held her fast. Panic-stricken, her hands swept downwards to free herself, and then she saw Manuel lying on the ground and realised who held her.

"He – he isn't dead?" she stammered.

Adam's eyes scanned her distraught face and for a brief moment his fingers touched her cheeks. He could not see the marks on her face in the half-light, but he had witnessed the struggle.

"No. Are you all right?"

"Yes," Maria Elena said breathlessly. As Adam bent over her unconscious brother, she cried out in alarm. "Don't kill him, Adam. Leave him here for my father to find."

He straightened, his mouth tightening.

"I don't dirk unconscious men, I was merely making sure we won't be followed for a while." He took her arm and propelled her along the path adding ironically,

"Besides, I've already killed one man in defence of your honour, I don't think the Queen would accept another death on your behalf."

Maria Elena did not breathe freely again until their carriage was some miles away. Her father would not give chase now, she thought, relaxing back in her seat.

"What did your brother want?" Adam asked, from the shadows in the corner.

"He was angry because I had not been to see him."

"And these plans he mentioned?"

So he had heard. Maria Elena shook her head in a silent answer.

"Where the devil did Francis go?"

"I asked him to leave me. He could hardly refuse. If you had not been otherwise engaged, Manuel would not have dared to show himself," Maria Elena said accusingly, and she could not hide the bitterness in her tone. "She is very beautiful – your mi – Lady Caroline."

"Why didn't you say my mistress?" Adam replied. "Yes, she is."

"Do you love her?"

"How many more times must I tell you not to use that word to me? I've had many women and loved none of them. I don't intend the situation should alter. Caroline has never meant anything to me – and now she knows I'll never see her again. You didn't witness a touching reunion, but a parting. Did you know she tried to keep me from you that night?"

"Yes. Sir Thomas told me," Maria Elena said.

"It's snowing again," Adam said suddenly, staring out of the carriage at the heavy flakes falling past the window. It was a pleasant night despite the crispness of the air, and the ache in his head left by too much wine had quickly dispersed.

"I'm cold." Maria Elena shivered and tucked her rug more firmly about her knees. "Can the driver go faster?"

"Not unless you want the horses to slip on the ice and

break their legs, and us to end up in an upside-down coach," Adam drawled. "Here, have my rug."

He leaned forward in his seat holding it out to her. The carriage jolted violently and he was thrown hard against her. His face brushed hers and his nostrils were filled with the sweet perfume of her hair.

The contact, brief though it was, proved sufficient to arouse his manhood. He had forgotten how soft and warm her body could be, and the pleasure he had gained from their short, tempestuous relationship. It had been over two months since he last made love to her – not since that wild night aboard the *Nemesis* before they set out for London. For the first time in his life he allowed passion to overrule judgement.

His mouth sought and found hers in the darkness, exploring it with a hunger so unexpected and so savage that Maria Elena had neither the strength nor the inclination to resist him. Her lips parted beneath his and her body responded instantly to the caresses of the hands which could be so cruel, yet at that moment were so gentle that they easily made her forget those other times.

"Adam. . . ."

"Be quiet."

"Are you drunk?"

Maria Elena raised her head and asked the question of the silent man whose arms still held her against him. The shadowy face above her smiled. She expected anger for such impertinence, but none came.

"No."

"Then why?"

"You look very beautiful tonight and I am feeling unusually human."

"Oh!" Maria Elena felt sick with disappointment.

"It must always be this way with us from now on," Adam said softly.

"If you wish it."

"Never betray me, Maria Elena, not even in your thoughts."

Maria Elena did not question this sudden change; his motives were his own concern. He had sent his mistress away and come to her again. In time he might even come to care for her just a little.

Adam sat up and lifted her away from him and she became aware he was laughing – silently and uncontrollably.

"It's permissible to seduce a mistress or even another man's wife in the back of a carriage, but I've never heard of a husband seducing his own wife in one before."

Maria Elena was grateful for the darkness of the interior, making it impossible for him to see her crimson cheeks as he tucked the rugs securely around her.

It was four o'clock as the carriage turned into the driveway at St. James's. Maria Elena was tired, but happy. She felt as if there were clouds beneath her feet. The house was quiet and all in darkness as they entered, except for a single candelabrum on the wood box, which Jamie always left burning whenever Adam went out. It had been a custom in the old house, Adam remembered as he picked it up, and found himself wondering how his wife would take to the bleak, beautiful Highlands of Scotland.

"I gave the servants the evening off," he said, "including your maid. The Queen's supper parties invariably last into the small hours."

They mounted the stairs together. To Maria Elena's surprise he led her past her bedroom and up a narrow flight of stairs at the end of the gallery, leading to a part of the house she did not know. Instinctively she knew that he was taking her to the attic.

It was a small room with low-slung beams which forced her to duck her head as she entered and wispy spiders' webs which brushed her face and tangled in her hair. Everything was covered in dust. The hem of her lovely gown trailed in inches of dirt, but she was too preoccupied to notice.

"No one is allowed up here. I keep the only key," Adam said glancing around him.

He held the candelabrum high for her to see the objects strewn about the room. A rusted target, a claymore suspended from a beam by a rotting cord – odd pieces of furniture, including a worn wooden bench, and beside it a heavily padlocked chest. Adam took off his cloak and spread it over the dusty bench.

"Come and sit down."

"Why have you brought me here?"

She loosened her cloak and allowed it to fall from her shoulders as she sat down. The candlelight picked out the intricately woven silver thread in the skirt of her gown and danced tantalisingly over the diamonds at her throat.

"To show you what manner of man you love."

He unlocked the chest and raised the lid almost reverently. He had cared for the contents for so long and so diligently. Not even his faithful Jamie had ever been in this room with him, to share his precious memories and re-live the past.

Maria Elena peered over his shoulder into the chest. She saw portraits with heavy gold frames and weapons, all of which bore the MacDonald crest. Adam's crest. She had seen it many times since that first day aboard the *San Cristobal*. A coat of arms was nailed over the main entrance to the house, another over the fireplace in his study. He was proud of his name – his heritage – no wonder he hated his mother for dishonouring everything he held dear.

"Were those your parents?" she asked softly, pointing to a miniature portrait of a man and woman in a tiny silver frame.

"Yes. My father, God rest his soul, and my beautiful, treacherous whore of a mother."

She took it from his unresisting grasp and stared down Father and son were almost twins.

"What was her name?"

"Sarah."

Maria Elena said the name to herself quietly. The woman in the portrait had red hair and soft hazel eyes. She wore a ruby on a gold chain around her neck. Maria Elena knew she could never have seen her before, yet somehow the face was familiar. It was not the face of an adulteress – a whore, as Adam called her.

"My father and I spent many months at sea, I suppose she grew lonely," Adam answered the unspoken question in her eyes. "But, good God, that didn't give her the right to take a lover! I heard talk in the village and had it out with her. She laughed in my face. I told her that if she betrayed my father, I'd kill her. She was gone the next time we came home. Jamie was being cared for by some of our kinsmen in the next glen after Luis Choulqueras had left him for dead. Our house had been razed to the ground and no one else was alive." Anger burned in his eyes as the memory grew clearer. "A dozen servants were slaughtered and the women not spared beforehand."

"Why did you not tell me this earlier?" Maria Elena asked in horror.

"Would you have believed me? It took Wyndham to make you realise that you were and always will be a pawn in your father's eyes."

"Did you see her again – your mother?"

"Once. We followed her to Spain. My father went to forgive her – I went to kill her. We were caught coming ashore and taken to the Don. She was there, standing behind his chair. I remember thinking how pale she looked and hoping the bastard had hurt her. She wouldn't come back, of course, not even when my father begged her. I lost my head and tried to kill her, that's when Manuel did this."

Adam touched the scar on his cheek. In the candlelight it showed suddenly red and ugly. "Six men held me down while he tried out a new dagger – and she watched. We escaped after four months in a pest-ridden hole with scarcely enough food to keep a mouse alive. Until he was killed some years later, my father and I attacked every ship of the Choulqueras line we came across. On his grave I swore I wouldn't rest until Luis Choulqueras and his son were dead."

Maria Elena's fingers tightened around the frame in her lap.

"And your mother?"

"Like all whores, her usefulness was soon over. Two years later she died of a fever in some pest-ridden brothel along the coast. She went there after your father threw her out."

"Poor woman."

"She got what she deserved."

"No, Adam. No woman deserves to be treated like that because she falls in love with the wrong man. These past weeks have taught me much about my father's character, and I am sure your mother suffered many times over for her mistake."

"Are you asking me to forgive and forget?"

"No, not now; in time you may. Try at least to stop hating a foolish, lonely woman who chased a dream and died more alone than she had ever been before – and probably very frightened."

"Somehow I've never thought of her like that," Adam said with a frown. Taking the painted miniature from her he replaced it in the chest and closed the lid. "Now you know my sordid family history and why I'm going to kill your father and Manuel. Can you still truthfully say you love me?"

"Yes," Maria Elena said quickly. "I accept the fact that you must grow tired of me and toss me aside exactly as my father did your mother – it's inevitable, but it doesn't matter. You have given me this moment and I am very happy."

Adam caught her by the shoulders, his fingers digging painfully into the soft skin, but he did not seem to notice.

"You little fool, why do you make me hurt you? I shall never love you, don't you see I can't? You're beautiful, desirable – and God help me, I enjoy sleeping with you, but that's all. There will never be anything else."

He threw the brutal words at her angrily, but no tears came, no reproaches. She was his for as long as he wanted her. If only she knew the ache in his heart every time he looked at her, Adam thought. Would she welcome his hands on her when they were stained with the blood of her father and brother?

Slowly he released her and stepped back, his face impassive.

"Remember it was your choice."

The crude scaffold on which Mary, Queen of Scotland was to die stood in the middle of the Great Hall in Fotheringay. The block was draped with a black cloth, so was the low stool beside it and the cushion. It was eight o'clock on the morning of February the eighth. More than two hundred spectators had come to watch Elizabeth's cousin die, but to Mary, when she came into the room, there was no one. She was alone with God. There was a gasp of horror as the executioner and his attendants moved forward and despite Mary's quiet protests, disrobed her. Beneath her sombre black gown she was clothed in a scarlet shift. It was as if she was covered in blood.

Many of the silent watchers had expected, indeed had hoped, to see her beg for mercy – to plead for her life from her Protestant cousin – but they were disappointed. Mary Stuart went to her death a Queen – a wronged woman – and a devout Catholic until the last breath was drawn, and as they watched, there were those who asked themselves, was this not wrong? She was a Queen after all.

The slender figure in red knelt before the block, serene, praying softly, ignoring the loud voice of the Dean of

Peterborough at the edge of the scaffold, calling to her to repent of her sins before she was condemned to everlasting damnation in the fires of Hell.

The chief executioner, although from the Tower of London and quite used to despatching people to the hereafter, was so unnerved by the figure kneeling before him in quiet acceptance of her fate, that it took not one but three blows of the axe to sever the head of Mary, and thus end years of misery and humiliation.

"There'll be the devil to pay for this piece of work," Francis Drake said fiercely. "A month, no more, and I swear we'll have every Catholic in England clamouring to Philip's banner."

Adam looked over the rim of his goblet to where his friend sprawled in the opposite chair, his face flushed with wine. They were in his study enjoying the Highland whisky Jamie had left out for them before he went to bed. Maria Elena had not dined with them. Adam knew the death of Mary Stuart had greatly upset her and she had been crying most of the day, but he suspected that there was also something else preying on her mind. The realisation the unfortunate execution must force her to make a last stand against her father's domination, perhaps. He gave orders that all her meals were to be served in her rooms and that she was not to be disturbed.

"Are you including me?" he asked amusedly.

Drake's eyes fixed themselves on his smiling face.

"No – not you."

"My wife then?"

"She's a Catholic."

"So am I."

"Damn it, man, she's Spanish."

"And she'll do nothing to endanger my life, I assure you."

"I wish I felt as confident," Drake answered, scowling.

"You worry too much." Adam leaned forward and

replenished their glasses. "Maria Elena is not implicated in this plot you speak of. It's the truth, believe me."

"I do, but I can't speak for others. Two hours after the death of Mary, the Don despatched three messengers. One to the Duke of Alba in the Netherlands, one to Philip of Spain, and the last. . . ."

"Yes, Francis?"

"He came here to this house. I doubt if he came to see you, for you were on board the *Nemesis* until dark."

Adam's eyes narrowed sharply.

"Is my house being watched?"

"Not your house, nor you – but your wife. It's Lord Burleigh's idea. She was to have married Wyndham, Adam, and you know why. She was payment for his men and money. Burleigh suggested you," Francis broke off, his face growing even redder, "but I squashed it at once."

"That I took her as payment for my services. Is that what he thinks?" Adam's voice was dangerously low – a warning Drake knew only too well. He stared into the hard brown face and wished with all his heart that Adam MacDonald had never returned to England.

"It's possible you may be implicated," he said worriedly. "Certain people who don't like you, and believe me there are many of those, are questioning the logic of your marriage to the daughter of a man you profess to hate deeply. And after bringing her to the Queen's supper party, it's obvious to everyone that the girl means something to you." He paused waiting for a denial, but none came.

"What do you suggest, my friend?"

"Get her aboard the *Nemesis* and leave before it's too late. When the Don's messengers return from Spain and the Netherlands they will be intercepted. God help us if there's to be an invasion. Heads will roll, and your wife's will certainly be one of them."

It was well into the early hours of the morning before Drake took his leave. Adam climbed the stairs to his bedroom in a thoughtful frame of mind. The time had come for him to make a choice. To stay and pursue his revenge could perhaps lose him his wife. To go would mean abandoning for ever any hope of killing his two worst enemies. Almost to the top of the stairs, he stopped, turned and went down to his study where he remained until dawn writing letters.

The days slipped by into weeks without incident. Francis Drake shut his ears to the whispered rumours and came often to dine at the MacDonald house. Nothing would induce him to believe that Adam was involved in a plot against the Queen, any more than he found it possible to think of Maria Elena as a dangerous conspirator.

The long days of uncertainty were slowly taking their toll of Maria Elena's strength. She had grown considerably thinner and the dark smudges beneath her eyes betrayed many a sleepless night. As he looked at her down the length of the dining-table, Adam was glad she would soon have the benefit of good Highland air to put the colour back into her cheeks. In three months she would have forgotten the pain and bitterness of old wounds. He prayed that the return to his old home would serve as well for him.

As the evening drew to a close Adam rang for Jamie to bring the wine he had kept back for the special moment.

"What's this?" Drake demanded, smiling.

"A surprise," Adam murmured. "I'm taking your advice and going away."

Maria Elena's fingers strayed to her throat and stayed there. The shock of his words momentarily robbed her of all breath.

"All my business has been taken care of," Adam went on. "The *Nemesis* is being prepared for sea at this moment. We shall leave around the end of the week."

Francis raised his goblet, his face alight with pleasure.

"God speed, my friend and a safe journey. Don't forget

to send me an invitation to the christening of your first son."

Maria Elena's eyes searched his face, but she saw nothing there to tell her he suspected that she was with child. She was not sure herself yet. She was under a strain and her health was not good. If the sickness continued, she had told Ninetta that morning, she would consult a doctor. It would have to wait now until she was in Scotland, and by then she would be sure. What a wonderful homecoming gift it would be for Adam!

She joined in the toast and her hand shook as she raised the glass to her lips. Adam looked at her intently and for a moment she thought he might comment on her nervousness, but he only smiled and continued talking to his friend.

The waiting was over. He was taking her with him, freeing her completely from the family chains which bound her. Neither Manuel nor her father would intrude into her world ever again to threaten her peace of mind.

She was to be Adam MacDonald's true wife – the mistress of his home. Her eyes glowed as she listened to him describing how it was being rebuilt for their return. He did not love her, but he had come to respect her and to accept her love without question. She would be a good wife to him, bear his children and make his friends welcome in their home and it was just possible, something other than respect would grow as the years passed.

While Adam was saying his farewells to Francis Drake in the hall, Maria Elena went into the drawing-room and sat down in a chair before the dying fire.

"Shall I make up the fire for ye, mistress?"

She raised her head to look at the old retainer at her elbow. He moved with the stealth of a fox, and as usual she had not heard him come into the room.

"No, Jamie, the master and I will be retiring soon."

"Then if there is nothing else, I'll bid ye goodnight."

"Just one thing," Maria Elena said quietly. "I shall

need the guidance of someone like you when we reach Scotland. Everything will be so strange and I want very much to please Adam. Why can't we be friends?"

"I was not aware we were anything else," Jamie answered, and the sour features softened almost into a smile. "Ye have made him happy despite everything, and I'm grateful to ye for it."

"Am I only to have gratitude? He has your love and devotion."

"If ye ever need help, ye will not have far to look for it. Goodnight, mistress."

"And what was Jamie grinning about?" Adam asked when he came into the room a moment later.

"I think we are friends at last," Maria Elena said, pleased that she had found enough courage to speak her mind.

"The old rogue has been waiting to speak to you for months, but he was afraid you'd snub him." Adam halted by her chair and smiled. "What do you think of my surprise?"

"I only hope I shall not disappoint you."

"In what way could you do that after all this time? You needn't be afraid of being lonely, despite the fact our nearest neighbours are twenty miles away. We'll have a ball as soon as the house is in better repair and I'll introduce you to everyone." Now that the final decision had been made he was impatient to show her his wild domain.

"But what if they don't want to meet me?" Maria Elena questioned. "They have no more reason to like Spaniards than you. What if they choose not to come – your friends will be lost because of me and then you will despise me for being a burden."

"A burden," Adam echoed and his face darkened. "You're my wife, not my mistress. My friends will come to our house, have no fear of that, and when they see how content I am, they'll envy me." Bending forward he caught her hands and drew her up against him. "Put these foolish thoughts out of your head. This is going to be the start of a new life for us both."

"And my father – Manuel? What of them?"

"They can go to the devil. We are going to Scotland," he returned in a low, fierce tone. And then, more gently, "You are everything a man could wish for in a woman. Who knows that better than I? We shall be free and happy, Maria Elena, and our children will grow up in an atmosphere that does not contain hatred and suspicion."

Maria Elena bit back the impulse to confide her suspicions to him. If she was not pregnant, the disappointment would be too great to bear now.

"I promised my father I'd marry some day and ensure that the MacDonalds of Glenmuir didn't die out with me. I made the promise cold-bloodedly, never believing I'd see the old place again. I'm glad I can keep my word after all – and with the promise of a future far richer than I deserve." Adam's arm moved around her shoulders and for a while he stared at her in silence. Then with a laugh, "Can you be packed by the end of the week?"

"By tomorrow, if you wish it."

"Why not? There's nothing to keep us here."

They went upstairs – not to Maria Elena's bedroom, but to her husband's. She rarely slept in her own bed any more. How different his love-making had become since that strange soul-baring night in the attic. More demanding, yet gentler. Always it seemed to Maria Elena that he set out to make her lose herself in the act – to forget he did not love her – and always in the end he, too, was lost. The ultimate union brought with it not only pleasure, but satisfaction such as she had never known before and utter contentment. Afterwards, when she lay in a half-sleep beside him, Adam reached out and drew her against him, cradling her head against his shoulder. Maria Elena fell asleep with the soft touch of his lips against her cheek.

"I must leave you in Jamie's capable hands, we sail in three hours," Adam said. "Are you sure you're all right?"

"It is only excitement," Maria Elena protested.

She sat on the edge of the couch in her sitting-room, trying hard to control the nausea which had thankfully subsided before Adam came into the room.

"And no breakfast," Ninetta declared behind her.

Adam frowned.

"Rectify it this instant. You are not to leave this house without some food inside you," he said to Maria Elena. "Is that clear?"

"Yes, Adam."

He bent over her and lightly kissed her pale cheeks. It was a gentle caress and Maria Elena saw the pleasure which leapt to his eyes as she returned the kiss, but on his mouth.

"If I remember correctly you were not a very good sailor the last time you were on board the *Nemesis*," he murmured. "I'd like this trip to be a better one."

When he had gone Maria Elena wandered through the house taking a final look at her home of the last four months. She did not feel sorrow at leaving it, but relief. She wondered if news of her departure had reached her father. Since she had burnt the last letter from him and sent his messenger back with a stinging reply, she had heard nothing more and had begun to believe that he had at last excluded her from his plans.

Ninetta brought her breakfast tray into the study and made her sit down, ignoring her mistress's grimace at the full plate of food.

"Have you finished all the packing, Ninetta?"

"Paco is fastening the last of the cases."

"Isn't it time you married that young man?" Maria Elena teased.

"Oh, yes, please! The master has promised us a house of our own in Scotland and land." Ninetta's face was a picture of joy. It was important for her to have Maria Elena's blessing.

Leaving her to eat her breakfast, she ran upstairs to her room and flung her arms around Paco's neck. He had been busy on the *Nemesis* all night and had missed his usual rendezvous with her. Six hours had seemed like six days for them both.

"When can we be married," Ninetta laughed, "today? Tomorrow? Oh, soon!"

"You little minx, what game are you playing now? Only yesterday you wanted to wait until we were in Scotland."

"I don't want to wait any longer."

She broke away as he bent to kiss her and for a moment Paco allowed her to evade his outstretched hands, laughing and chasing her around the cases on the floor.

"Enough, my girl. You've had your fun and I've been waiting all night for this."

He caught her by the waist, pressing her back against the wall beside the window and held her fast with the full weight of his body.

"Paco – no – I have not finished my work."

Ninetta protested only half-heartedly. Paco's kisses silenced her and they stood locked in a passionate embrace. At last his mouth came away from hers and she leaned against him, waiting for him to lift her on to the bed. Her eyes flew open in alarm as he swore savagely. She saw that he was staring out of the window, down into the courtyard and the expression on his face frightened her.

"What is it?"

"Don Luis and that son of Satan – Manuel. By all the saints, I swear I've just seen them sneaking into the house."

CHAPTER TEN

"WHAT do you want?"

Maria Elena stood in the middle of the study, her face white and shocked as she stared at her father and brother. She had been happily singing to herself as she prepared to go upstairs and then they had appeared in the doorway, swords drawn, their attitudes menacing. This was no farewell visit. Don Luis' face was unreadable, but beside him Manuel's dark eyes glittered with hate as he stared at his sister. There was blood on one of his cheeks and his clothes were ripped in several places.

"For the love of God, answer me," Maria Elena cried. "Why are you here?"

"Our cause is lost, the Queen knows everything. The messenger from King Philip was intercepted and tortured. Many of our friends have already been arrested. We are being sought at this very moment."

Luis Choulqueras strode about the room as he spoke, peering cautiously out of the windows. Eventually satisfying himself that they had not been followed, he sheathed his weapon and ordered Manuel to do likewise.

"What if a servant comes?" Manuel demanded.

"Maria Elena will not betray us. She's going to help us."

Maria Elena groped for a chair and sat down.

"I won't help you. I won't." She beat a tiny clenched fist on the top of the polished table. "I have finished with you. Please, go away and leave me alone."

"I'll see you dead first," Manuel growled.

"Kill me then, but I won't lift a finger to help you."

"Then we shall kill MacDonald as well," Don Luis said

in a deadly tone. "Did you think you could slip away without my knowing, you stupid girl?"

"Then why have you not tried to stop me?"

"If you were of the least importance to me, I should have had my men bring you to me before now. You think with your heart, not your head. You were more of a danger to us than an asset. But now it seems you can render me one last service before we part company. You will persuade your husband to give us safe passage to the Netherlands – or you will never see each other again. Manuel will kill you here, and then I shall allow him to use his own brand of persuasion on MacDonald. He would like that, would you?"

"No – no!" Maria Elena cried starting to her feet. "What must I do?"

"We shall all go to the *Nemesis*. The sight of you with us should make MacDonald agreeable."

"Very well." Maria Elena said resignedly. She had no other choice, she had to trust them. If only Manuel would not look at her with such animosity in his expression.

"Where are you going?" he caught her wrist as she moved past him.

"To fetch my cloak."

"I will come with you."

They were almost to the top of the stairs when there came a thunderous knocking at the front door. Manuel pushed her back against the balustrade and drew his sword. Luis Choulqueras appeared below them, sword in hand.

"Soldiers! Out the back way – hurry!"

Maria Elena tried to run upstairs, but her brother caught her around the waist and dragged her bodily downstairs.

"What do we do with this traitress?"

"Leave her, your life is more important to me. Her name will be sufficient to send her to the Tower," his father retorted.

The door shuddered under heavy blows and he turned and ran towards the servants' quarters.

Manuel dragged Maria Elena away from the wall with a terrible smile. Fear for his own safety was overcome by the hatred he had for this pale-faced girl before him.

"You will not live to see Scotland, sister – or the Tower."

Maria Elena cried out and closed her eyes as his sword flashed down towards her. She heard a grunt of pain, and his hold on her slackened and fell away. She opened her eyes on to Paco's smiling face and looked down to find her brother dead at her feet, a knife in his back.

"It was for Ninetta," Paco said simply.

Maria Elena was too overcome to reply. She allowed him to lead her into the drawing-room, unaware of the soldiers rushing past her.

"My father – he will go to the *Nemesis* – he will kill Adam," she faltered.

"No, señora, I think not." Paco looked up at the silent figure in the doorway.

"Don Luis is dead," Francis Drake said curtly. "Maria Elena Choulqueras, in the name of our gracious Queen, Elizabeth of England, I arrest you on a charge of high treason."

"And my husband?" Maria Elena's voice was hardly audible.

"He has been confined aboard his ship. He sails with the tide, never to set foot in England again under penalty of death." Drake's cold manner relented for an instant. "I have orders to speed him on his way personally. Have you a message for him?"

Maria Elena shook her head and he saw her eyes were filled with tears. At that moment he was convinced of her innocence.

"No, he is free of me now. Let him go in peace."

Maria Elena's audience with Elizabeth was brief and painless. She rode to the palace in a closed carriage and was shown into the Queen's presence with two armed guards behind her. The tight, angry face before her, with its glittering eyes, did not frighten her. She had made up her mind that her child would not be born in prison to be taken from her, nor would she suffer death for something she had not done.

"Have you nothing to say, girl?"

Elizabeth's voice thundered across the empty room at her, and behind Maria Elena the two guards winced. They had seen the Queen's tempers before.

"No, Your Majesty. Nothing."

The calmness of the girl before her sent Elizabeth into a rage. She threatened torture to make her speak, describing in detail the hideous instruments used which could break the strongest of men. Maria Elena's sereneness did not falter. The Queen could not hurt her. With Adam gone, no one could do that ever again. When Elizabeth's rage had subsided she said quietly but firmly, "With respect to Your Majesty, I consider it better to lose my head than to betray my father and lose my self-respect."

The audience came to an abrupt end. Elizabeth ordered her to be returned to the house to await her pleasure.

The house in St. James's was closely guarded. Maria Elena saw two soldiers on the main entrance, one in the garden, two patrolling the street and many more wandering in and out of the house, when she returned. Jamie took her cloak and gloves, his lined face drawn with anxiety. The poor lass looked worn out, he thought.

"Come, mistress, ye must rest. I've supper ready in ye're room. Wisht now, forget about the soldiers, come away upstairs."

It was not until she was upstairs that Maria Elena realised Ninetta was noticeably absent, and asked where she was.

"Ye are supposed to be here alone," Jamie said. "Captain Drake had everyone else put aboard the *Nemesis*."

"But you are here."

"Aye. I said I'd be near if ye ever needed help. That girl – yer maid told me about the child ye carry. I couldna' leave ye with a rabble of soldiers now, could I? Eat yer food like a good lass."

Maria Elena looked at him with trembling lips.

"Jamie – has he sailed yet?"

"Aye – three hours ago. Ye'd think he had the Queen's jewels aboard the way the ship was surrounded by soldiers."

"You should have gone with him. I'm as good as dead."

"The Queen may be English, but she's a woman," Jamie said frowning. "When ye tell her about the child. . . ."

"I don't intend to tell her. No – I will not be persuaded. Adam is safe, nothing else matters. Take the food away, Jamie, I am not hungry."

Jamie saw that her face was wet with tears as she went into the bedroom and closed the door behind her.

A sour-faced sergeant presented himself at the house not two hours later and demanded Maria Elena's presence. She came downstairs knowing in her heart that she was to hear bad news. She was to be taken to the Tower the following morning to await trial. She had heard tales of that terrible place where hundreds languished in dungeons below the ground, starved and forgotten, but better off by far than those who ended their days on the rack. She felt herself grow suddenly faint. The sergeant watched unmoved as Jamie came forward to help her back to her room.

Jamie set her gently down on the couch and brought her a glass of wine.

"Don't give up, mistress. I will be with ye whatever happens."

"They will not be taking me to that place," Maria Elena whispered. Her eyes flickered past him to the corner of the room she preserved as a chapel. "I know what I must do even though it be a sin. Leave me, dear Jamie. Save yourself while you can. You need have no more fears for me."

No explanation was necessary. Adam had told his steward of the poison ring she had once tried to use.

"No, mistress, ye can't."

"I must. Would you have me suffer torture instead?"

Jamie looked into her pale face and was silent. He had no right to deny her this escape, but it would not be easy to take the news to Adam in Scotland. He had hoped of the possibility of somehow smuggling her on board the *Nemesis*, but the ship had been so closely guarded that he had not even been able to get a message to Adam – or receive one.

"If ye need anything, ye have only to ring," he said and left her before she had time to see the tears streaming down over his cheeks. Once he had considered her an intruder – an enemy. Now he would gladly give his own life to save her.

Maria Elena picked up her glass of wine and went across to the tiny statue of the Madonna standing in the candlelit alcove. She put it down on the table and took something from the bodice of her dress – something which flashed in the candlelight. Opening the ring, she emptied the quantity of white powder into the glass. It had taken an hour of careful searching to find where Adam had hidden it in his study.

She was so lost in prayer some time later that she neither heard the quiet knocking on the door, nor heard it open behind her.

"Señora."

She turned and rose stiffly to her feet, knowing fear as she had never known it before at the sight of the black-robed figure before her – and behind the priest, armed soldiers.

"Has my time come? I was told tomorrow," she whispered.

"It is the Queen's wish you be transported under cover of darkness," the priest said. His face was hidden by a large cowl.

Jamie pushed past the soldiers, his face tight with anger.

"Get out, ye heathen cur, and let the lass be alone with the priest," he said, and slammed the door so that Maria Elena and her companion were alone.

"Will you give me your blessing, Father?" she asked sinking down on her knees before him.

Lean, strong hands fastened over her shoulders and drew her to her feet. She looked up and stared disbelievingly into the smiling face she knew so well, and from a far-off distance heard Adam chuckle.

"I'll give you my soul if you ask me, lass, but let's get away from here first."

"But – you sailed with the *Nemesis*!"

"I did – and before she reached the open sea, I was with the Duchess hiring men to get you out of here." His dark eyes searched her face. "They haven't touched you?"

"No – I am to be taken to the Tower tomorrow."

"Thank God I came in time."

"Why didn't you save yourself while you could? If you are found helping me. . . ."

"Why? Because I love you. I've never loved another woman in my life. Is that reason enough for you, my little witch?"

The softly spoken confession shattered the final barriers between them and brought tears rushing to Maria Elena's eyes. With a sob she turned her face into his shoulder and wept.

Adam held her close against him for a long while, then gently put her from him.

"You must do exactly as I say. Do you understand?"

"Yes, Adam."

He smiled and kissed her on each wet cheek. He dared not kiss her mouth.

"You always were the most obedient woman I've known," he teased.

"Where are we going?"

"Once we are safely out of here – to the Duchess's place. Have you enough strength to go through with it?" His fingers traced the path of a tear down her cheek. "My poor darling, you look exhausted."

Maria Elena thought of the child within her and quickly nodded. She must give him no reason to endanger his life further by taking extra precautions.

"Fetch a warm cloak, we have very little time. I'll pack a small bag; we must convince the soldiers you are really going to the Tower."

"Ninetta has already done that. I'll fetch it."

He followed her to the door of the bedroom where his attention was arrested by the objects on the table beside which Maria Elena had been praying. When she rejoined him the look on his face told her that he had guessed her intentions.

"I am a coward," she said shakily. "I could not stand torture, and with you gone there was no reason to prolong my existence."

Adam said nothing, but she saw his face pale considerably. Wordlessly he bent and kissed her fiercely on the lips, then quickly turned away, adjusting the cowl over his face again.

There were three soldiers at the end of the corridor when he stepped outside, and Jamie, who was waiting immediately outside the door.

"Are the men downstairs taken care of?" he murmured.

"Aye – snoring their heads off. What was yon mixture I gave them?"

"A concoction of the Duchess's – bless her. Maria Elena, hold on to Jamie's arm. My men are waiting in the garden." She saw a flash of steel as he slid his dirk into the sleeve of his habit. "Give me a moment, then follow."

He moved slowly towards the watching soldiers, his head downbent over an open prayer-book. Jamie picked up Maria Elena's hand-trunk, into which she had hastily pushed her jewel-case. The contents could be used as bribes if necessary.

"He loves me," she whispered. "He loves me, Jamie."

"I could have told ye that months ago. I knew it before he did. Have ye told him about the child?"

"No – not until we are safe. I am afraid he would take too many risks for my sake. You must not tell him."

"Nay, I'll leave that pleasure to ye. Come now, walk slow and pretend to be crying. These scum have no stomach for tears and yon sentry in the garden will be so uncomfortable, he'll not look twice at us."

As they came out of the house into the cool night air and walked down the path which led to the river, Maria Elena understood. The solitary guard was a boy of eighteen or nineteen and at the sight of the heavily-cloaked woman crying into her handkerchief, he turned away and allowed them to pass after a cursory glance. Adam sat beside her in the boat, mumbling in a tone too low for anyone to understand as it was cast off from its moorings and headed out into the middle of the river.

"Row, you sons of Satan," he said in a sudden distinct tone. "If we're caught you'll be alongside me on the next rack."

His words gave strength to the bogus soldiers straining at the oars and soon the house slipped away into the darkness behind them. As soon as that happened uniforms were torn off and thrown into the river, weighed down by stones. Adam divested himself of the cumbersome robes and turned to smile into Maria Elena's white face.

"We're safe now, my darling. By tomorrow night we'll be on board the *Nemesis* and on our way home."

Scotland – she would see it after all. A sudden pain stabbed through her body, robbing her of all breath. And then another, this time so intense that she fainted.

Someone was bathing her face with a cool cloth – someone who smelt strongly of powder and cheap perfume. Maria Elena opened her eyes upon the Duchess's painted face.

"Adam!"

She attempted to sit up, but was firmly prevented from doing so.

"Be still. Do you want to lose the baby?" the Duchess said harshly.

"How do you know?"

"You little fool, I'm a woman, aren't I? I've had a son of my own." She drew back from the bed and Adam appeared in Maria Elena's vision. He knelt at her side and taking both her hands in his, held them to his lips.

"Why didn't you tell me?"

"I wanted us to be in Scotland first – in your father's house. It seemed right somehow."

An expression of great tenderness came into his eyes. Oblivious to Jamie or the silent figure of the Duchess, he took Maria Elena in his arms. The sight was too much for Sarah MacDonald who turned away and went unnoticed from the room. When she returned she brought with her a complete change of clothes for everyone.

"You'll travel with a group of actors," she told them, bundling Maria Elena's satin dress beneath the bed to be burnt later on. "It's unlikely you'll be missed until morning, and then they'll start searching the ships first. Are you sure the *Nemesis* will be waiting?" she queried looking at Adam.

"It's safely in our cove off the Cornish coast." He stepped towards the woman frowning. "It could be dangerous for you here now."

"You paid me well."

"No gold on earth can repay the help you've given me," Adam said gruffly. "My thanks, duchess. I won't forget. are you ready, Maria Elena?"

"I will come in a moment."

Maria Elena waited until her husband and jamie had gone, and then she unfastened the sapphire bracelet round her wrist and held it out to the duchess.

"Take it, please."

Sarah looked at her for a long while before she took it.

"You have a strange bond with my husband and because of it you have placed yourself in great danger. It was not for me, I know that, but I am still grateful," Maria Elena whispered. "Come with us — our house could be your home. It is the least we can do."

Sarah turned away, her face lined with pain. Upon an impulse she flung open the lid of her jewel-box and delved deep into the contents.

"When you and Adam are in Scotland and the heather is thick like a purple cloak on the hills behind the house, give him this and he'll tell you why I didn't come."

Maria Elena stared down at the huge ruby the Duchess pressed into her hand. She raised incredulous eyes to the powdered face. "I know why. He still has a portrait of you wearing this. He thinks you are dead."

"It's in your hands whether or not he knows the truth. You love him very much and you'll give him fine sons. Perhaps when the old house rings with the sound of children's laughter, the bitterness will leave him and he'll think of me sometimes." She took Maria Elena's arm and spun her around to the door. "We are wasting time, hurry."

Adam and Jamie were waiting in the courtyard outside. They looked no different from the other four men standing beside the heavily laden mummers' cart. A tall, slim youth stepped forward to make a sweeping bow before the two women.

"Will Shakespeare — this is the girl I spoke of. No dallying and no sweet words, lad, her husband stands behind you." The Duchess stepped back and surveyed everyone through narrowed eyes. "If you don't reach your ship, Adam MacDonald, it'll be no fault of mine," she said harshly, and turned back into the tavern.

Three days later the *Nemesis* slipped quietly out to sea and headed on a course for Scotland. The journey had been slow and uneventful, but no one breathed easily until the Cornish coastline faded into the distance behind them.

The bumpy ride had taken its toll of Maria Elena's strength and she was put to bed directly she reached the ship, to be fussed over by Ninetta who wept for hours upon seeing her safe and unharmed.

On their fourth night at sea Adam awoke to find that Maria Elena was no longer beside him. He leaned up on one elbow and saw her standing by the dressing table, staring down at her hands.

"What is it, *querida*? Are you feeling ill?"

"No – nothing like that. I could not sleep – I am too happy."

"Come back and let me warm you before you catch a chill," Adam murmured.

When they were happily settled in Scotland and the hate had gone out of him, she would tell him the truth, Maria Elena thought. Dropping the ruby back into the jewel-casket, she closed the lid and went back to bed.

Masquerade
Historical Romances

Intrigue excitement romance

Don't miss
May's
other enthralling Historical Romance title

THE ELUSIVE MARRIAGE
by Patricia Ormsby

It is only to be expected that the high-spirited Miss Cherryanne Devenish will embroil herself in a scrape when she takes her place in gossip-loving Regency society. But not even she can foresee the circumstances of her first meeting with the notorious Marquis of Shalford — when he bursts into her bedchamber at a wayside inn, seeking a vantage to shoot an escaped lioness!

After that encounter, Miss Devenish wants nothing more than to put the adventure — and the Marquis — out of her mind. Besides, he is destined to marry the rich and charming Honoria Winton, in order to repair his fortune. Circumstances, however, continue to throw the Marquis and Miss Devenish together, and more decorous courtships have lost their savour for her ...

You can obtain this title today from your local paperback retailer

Doctor Nurse Romances

and May's
stories of romantic relationships behind the scenes
of modern medical life are:

NURSE AT WHISPERING PINES
by Elizabeth Petty

The shock of being jilted had left Storm without the heart to continue her nursing career. Then she found that her sick grandmother needed her in Canada — and so did the uncompromising Clint Hawes...

WISH WITH THE CANDLES
by Betty Neels

There were plenty of girls with more glamour to offer a devastating Dutch surgeon than Sister Emma Hastings. Wasn't she wasting her time by falling in love with Justin Teylingen?

Order your copies today from your local paperback retailer

Masquerade
Historical Romances

Intrigue excitement romance

SATAN'S MOUNTAIN
by Kate Buchan

Even after the American Civil War, the mountains of Connecticut were riddled with superstition and fear — so Miss Helen Shaw, from Boston, discovered when she went there to claim the property she had inherited from her grandfather. And her cousin and fellow-heir, Robert Warren, was reputed to be in league with the devil . . .

DUEL OF LOVE
by Helen May

Cassandra Wells returned to Society only because she must chaperone her harum-scarum niece Susan. Unfortunately, the first person she met was Jonathan, Lord Verax, whose offer she had once spurned — and he seemed annoyingly willing to take her at her word, and pay court to Susan!

Look out for these titles in your local paperback shop from 13th June 1980

Masquerade
Historical Romances

Intrigue excitement romance

FOLLOW THE DRUM
by Judy Turner

To escape an arranged marriage, Barbara Campion fled from home determined to find her soldier sweetheart. Daringly disguised as a boy, she enlisted in the Rifle Brigade and followed the drum through Belgium to the Battle of Waterloo — under the command of the fascinating Captain Alleyn ...

STOLEN INHERITANCE
by Anne Madden

Deborah Wyngarde's journey to London with her brother Philip, to claim their inheritance from the newly-restored King Charles II, seemed wasted when they were scorned as impostors. And Deborah had meanwhile lost her heart to the Earl of Mulgarth — whom even his sister declared to be a hardened rake!

ABIGAIL'S QUEST
by Lois Mason

Abigail's father had disappeared — swallowed up in the gold rush to New Zealand in 1862. On her quest to look for him, she found herself married to Rob Sinclair — a near-stranger!

These titles are still available through your local paperback retailer